"Are you g[...]

Karen asked the que[...]
was glad she didn't [...]

"Yes. Your uncle Brady and I are going to get married on Friday, so you can stay here."

Karen's eyes went wide and then filled with tears. In an attempt to soothe her Dana said, "I know this is all happening very fast. But we're not going to try to be your mom and dad."

Karen shook her head. "I used to pray that you'd be our mother. You were always so nice to us. I loved my momma, but she didn't love us back."

Dana didn't know what to say. This sweet girl was giving so much of herself, but Dana couldn't do the same. Brady kept telling her this was only temporary. If she gave her love to the children and then had to watch them walk away, she might never recover. How was she ever going to resist these three girls?

Dear Reader,

This book started with a newspaper article my late father
had saved for me about a one-room schoolhouse. "Hey,
look at this, Sus," he said with a grin. "Wouldn't this be a
great story?" Unfortunately, my father isn't here to witness
his kernel of an idea come to fruition, but I still like to
thank him for his inspiration, which led to this story.

Now take three abandoned children starving for love, a
schoolteacher reluctant to ever become attached to any of
her students again and a deputy sheriff racked with guilt
because he believes the children's plight is the result of
actions he took several years before. Mix them all together,
stir in generous amounts of chaos, unresolved feelings and
long-kept secrets and bake with a marriage of convenience.
Season with healing and forgiveness. Is this the recipe to
make a family?

Join Dana Ritchie and Brady Moore as they wade through
this crazy thing we call life and together discover that two
are stronger than one. You—my readers—mean everything
to me, and I love to hear from you. You can write to me at
P.O. Box 2883, Los Banos, CA 93635 or by e-mail at
susfloyd@yahoo.com.

Sincerely,

Susan Floyd

Books by Susan Floyd

HARLEQUIN SUPERROMANCE

My Three Girls
Susan Floyd

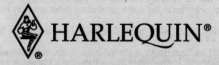

HARLEQUIN®

TORONTO • NEW YORK • LONDON
AMSTERDAM • PARIS • SYDNEY • HAMBURG
STOCKHOLM • ATHENS • TOKYO • MILAN • MADRID
PRAGUE • WARSAW • BUDAPEST • AUCKLAND

ISBN 0-373-71097-6

MY THREE GIRLS

Copyright © 2002 by Susan Kimoto.

This edition published by arrangement with Harlequin Books S.A.

Visit us at www.eHarlequin.com

Printed in U.S.A.

This book took the work of several people from San Benito, Monterey and Merced Counties.

Heartfelt thanks to:
Monterey County deputy sheriffs
Greg Liskey, Mike Richards, Larry Robinson
and Jeff Stiarwalt (for the adventurous "ride along").

Merced County deputy sheriffs
Tomas Cavallero and Richard St. Marie (for brainstorming
at the Los Banos Campus Career Fair).

Panoche Elementary School District, San Benito County
Ginger Gardner, Teacher and Principal
Elsa Rodriguez, Teacher's Aide, Cook, Janitor
and Groundskeeper

Mario Bencomo, 5th grade
Aaron Blanco, 7th grade
Ian Blanco, 5th grade
Dustin Borba, 1st grade
Alyssa Cabral, 4th grade
Chantelle Lippert, 7th grade
Jacob Lippert, 6th grade
Zoa Lopez, 6th grade
Tristan Redondo, 2nd grade

This is dedicated to all my students at Merced College,
Los Banos Campus, who have brainstormed titles, offered
plotting advice and understood the value of a "redo."

CHAPTER ONE

DANA TUGGED at the collar of her sleeveless cotton dress, feeling a damp film of sweat on her sternum. Indian summer in California's Panoche Valley was just more of the same—dry and brittle, the victim of a scorching summer. Cattle on the rolling hills searched for shade and found it at the chain-link border of a one-room schoolhouse, a green oasis of non-native shade trees nestled in a valley of brown.

Dana glanced at the large clock on the wall. It was nearly six on a Friday, but it wasn't strange that she was still at work. When she was twenty-four, Dana had taken on the role of principal and teacher at one of the smallest schools in California's Central Valley, a job that took someone who was either a loner or a certified workaholic.

Dana was both.

For the past five years, she'd embraced the isolation, hoping that work and the dark, still nights could wrap her in a protective blanket. It hadn't always been that way. There was a time, new teaching credentials in hand, she had taught in an urban school filled with low-income children even more thirsty for the safety school offered than for the subsidized cartons of milk. She'd had colleagues then, a few she might call friends, but those faces were a blur now. The only face she saw with heartbreaking regularity was the one she tried not to see, the one permanently imprinted in her vision like a sunspot. Round cheeks, clear brown eyes, a shock of black hair.

Dana reached over and jerked down the shade. The temperature of her west-facing office dropped ten degrees. Now wasn't the time to be thinking about him, what he'd be like as a teenager. With brisk movements, she began to sort through the forms on her desk, prioritizing the night's work. Even though she only had twelve students, she needed to fill out the same reports that the larger schools did. Fire safety, student evacuation plans, building and lighting requirements.

If she filled out enough forms, if she buried herself in her work, the unbearable pain became a dull knot where her heart once was. That had been a successful strategy for five years, but now that the frenzy of developing lesson plans, organizing the school year and implementing the latest state-mandated curriculum had become more routine, the grief she'd thought she'd been able to sidestep dogged her relentlessly. Her mother had told her in her no-nonsense manner that the loss of a child, even if the child wasn't hers, was something that no one ever got over, and that she needed to face her grief rather than run away from it. Dana disagreed. Grief could be put off if one kept busy enough.

Which was why this situation was perfect for her. After all, how many people could boast of no commute, no neighbors, no true boss, except for the school board who supported every one of her efforts to update the small school? When she finished her day's work, which generally wasn't until nine or ten in the evening, she just walked fifty feet to the district-owned, two-bedroom cottage she called home, ate a sandwich or a bowl of cereal and flopped into bed. On Saturday, she would return to the schoolhouse to work on the endless list of minor repairs it needed. On Sunday, she would clean and set up the classroom for the following week. It was a wonderful system that had kept the terrible waves of depression at bay for years.

"Hellooo?" a singsong voice called.

Dana's head snapped up at the intrusion. No

one ever came onto the school property after school hours unless it was parents' night. But that only happened twice a year. She pushed away from her desk and poked her head up over the file cabinets.

"Hello? Miss Ritchie?"

Dana groaned when she recognized the person and the oh-too-sweet-voice at the same time. Beverly Moore. The only parent she had personality conflicts with. Maybe it was because Mrs. Moore was new and hadn't quite acquired small-school etiquette. Most of her parents traveled as far as forty miles to drop off their children, and Dana did what she could to accommodate their schedules, since they didn't have a lot of time for chitchatting. Most lived and worked on ranches or farms so rural that running water was a luxury. Like the school's, their electricity was gleaned from a generator. When the parents picked up their children at two-thirty, they were singleminded in their efforts to get back to their properties. Livestock needed to be fed, fences needed to be mended. Dana used the snatches of time before and after school to update them quickly on their children's progress or lack thereof.

Mrs. Moore, whose three daughters had enrolled at the last minute but made up a quarter of her class this year, was a parent of a different caliber. The family lived in a house just two miles from the school, and Beverly Moore seemed to believe that Dana was a built-in baby-sitter. Dana could count on the fact the Moore girls would be the first ones dropped off in the morning, sometimes an hour early, and the last ones picked up—often by two or three hours. They were occasionally dropped off on weekends so they could play on the school grounds, too.

Dana didn't appreciate the added responsibility, but the girls kept to themselves and weren't destructive in any way, so she let it slide. Eventually she'd become used to hearing Karen bark orders at her younger sisters, and Ollie, the youngest, scream with delight.

"Miss Ritchie?" The voice was getting closer, along with the distinct clicking of high heels.

Mrs. Moore's perfume reached Dana before she did.

Dana summoned a stiff smile and called, "Yes?" She stepped out from behind the file cabinets.

The other woman stopped short. "Oh! I'm so glad you're here. I knocked on your door, but when there wasn't an answer, I took the chance you'd be in the school. I saw your car, so I knew you hadn't gone anywhere.''

One good reason why Dana should park in the garage.

''What can I do for you?'' Dana said, her voice as crisp as she could make it. She even crossed her arms over her chest, hoping that Mrs. Moore was attuned to nonverbal communication.

No such luck.

''I need the biggest favor from you.'' She smiled as if Dana were her closest and dearest friend, then placed a manicured hand on Dana's forearm.

Dana worked not to flinch; she didn't want people touching her. She removed herself from the contact. All that did was give her a better look at the other woman's ensemble. The manicure, the heels, the perfume all set off an impeccable beige linen suit. Dana eyed the cream silk camisole with something that she might have called envy a lifetime ago. Despite the heat, Beverly Moore looked cool and composed. Dana felt every inch the dowdy schoolmarm.

''I know it's an imposition,'' Beverly continued, as if Dana's silence was consent, ''but I've been called out of town and I'm just not able to get a baby-sitter.''

"No." The word was out of her mouth before Dana could stop it.

Even Beverly looked taken aback. "No? You don't even know what I was going to ask."

"To baby-sit, maybe?" Dana raised an eyebrow, her voice dry.

Beverly had the grace to flush. "It would only be for the weekend." She spoke rapidly as if speed would convince Dana to grant her the favor.

"No." Dana had been down that road once before. First, it was baby-sitting, then foster care, then— "No!" She turned her back. "School is out for the weekend."

"It's a very important business conference I need to attend. I'll be back on Sunday."

Sunday? Dana didn't dare look at the woman in case eye contact would be considered assent. What would she do with the Moore girls for two whole days?

"I can pay—"

Dana turned, feeling her face get red. "I don't need money."

Beverly Moore shrugged, looking at Dana's clothes, her gaze fastening on Dana's serviceable shoes. "I'd make it worth your while."

"I don't think you could," Dana replied.

"Now, if you'll excuse me I have a great deal of work to do. I hope you find someone."

The woman's lipsticked mouth pinched tightly together, but finally she nodded and left, heels clicking across the linoleum. With the final bang of the closing door, Dana expelled the breath she was holding. Then she crossed the room and locked the door before settling back in her chair and picking up the form on the top of the pile. She studied the fine print and began to fill it out.

The front door handle rattled.

Dana's back stiffened. Surely Mrs. Moore couldn't be back.

"Miss Ritchie?" The voice came sailing toward her through the locked door, as cheerful as if they hadn't had the previous conversation. Dana stayed silent, hoping Mrs. Moore would think that she'd gone back to the house.

"I know you're in there," the woman said. "I know you haven't gone. The girls say you don't ever go anywhere."

Dana kept her head down and tried to concentrate on the form in front of her. Then a persistent knocking started.

How long could she keep that up? Eventually, her knuckles would be raw and—

"I'm going to keep knocking until you open

this door.'' Mrs. Moore was sounding rattled and the knocking changed to pounding.

Dana popped to her feet, angrier than she remembered being in a long time. She crossed to the door with several impatient steps. This was her private time. ''I *told* you—''

Mrs. Moore stood on the concrete entryway, this time with her daughters, Karen, Jean and little Ollie, positioned in front of her, all clutching small backpacks.

''Hi, Miss Ritchie.'' Karen spoke first, her voice uncertain as she glanced up at her mother.

''Mrs. Moore.'' Dana frowned.

''Bev. Call me Bev.'' She waved her hand toward her daughters. ''The girls want to thank you for agreeing to take them this weekend. They like you so much.''

Dana doubted that. The girls interacted as little as possible with the other children *and* her. The eleven-year-old, Karen, seemed to take exception to any attention that was paid to the younger girls, Jean, six, and Ollie, just five. They were well mannered, although Jean retreated so often to lengthy silences it was easy to forget that she spoke at all. Dana also noticed both Jean and Ollie had the curious habit of kicking the supply closet every time they passed by. The third time Dana had to wash off the scuff marks, she'd asked them not to do it. Jean had answered with a staring silence, and Ollie's eyes had filled with tears. The brief discussion hadn't saved her cabinet, though. The two girls simply kicked with more stealth.

"Uh, thank you, Miss Ritchie," Karen blurted, nudged by her mother. "We'll be very good."

"This is blackmail," Dana said to Mrs. Moore.

"I'm desperate or I wouldn't put you in this position," she said. From her voice and the way she glanced over her shoulder, it seemed to be the first truthful statement Beverly Moore had made.

"I'm sorry, but I can't take the girls." Dana was firm. She wasn't going to be railroaded into this duty. She wasn't the only option that Mrs. Moore had. She was just convenient. "You might consider taking them with you." With that, Dana shut the door and tried to lock it, but her hand was shaking so badly she couldn't turn the dead bolt properly. The knocking started again.

"Go away!" Dana muttered under her breath, eventually managing to lock the door. "Leave me alone." She put her hands over her ears and walked back to her office, then turned on her small radio to drown out the knocking. After a while, it stopped, but Dana's heart still kept pounding. She worked for two more futile hours, not really accomplishing anything.

She stared at the pile of work on her desk. Nothing said she had to finish it tonight. She would spend tomorrow morning making the repairs and reattack the pile in the afternoon. She had no other plans. She walked around the perimeter of the schoolroom, checking to make sure she'd turned off the computers. If she had her way, she'd never leave the schoolhouse. It gave her the comfort that her home didn't. Finally, she unlocked the front door and opened it. The air was cool, pleasant, a significant difference between summer and fall. In fact, Dana shivered in her sleeveless dress as she closed up. Movement caught her eye, and the motion sensor turned on a bright light.

Dana whirled. Surely the cattle hadn't pushed through the fence again. She'd have to call the rancher who owned them before they trampled the students' agriculture projects. She tried to focus on the movement in the deepening dusk. Since she was standing in the light, it was hard to see what was out there.

"Hi, Miss Ritchie," a small voice called.

"Karen?" Dana walked toward the voice.

"Yes, Miss Ritchie?" The voice was still uncertain, and Dana could swear she was holding back tears.

"What are you girls doing here?" Dana's eyes were becoming accustomed to the dark. She could make out three figures at the picnic table where the children ate lunch on nice days. Ollie was standing on the table, swaying from foot to foot. Karen and Jean huddled together on the bench.

"Momma said to wait and you'd take care of us," Ollie told her.

"Where is your mother?"

There was a long silence. Then Karen said, her voice brave, "She went to a conference. She said to tell you that we promise to be very good and that she'd be back Sunday afternoon."

Dana inhaled, warning bells going off in her head. This had to be against school policy. There had to be some rule about keeping students at her personal residence. If there wasn't, there should be. If Beverly Moore was going to leave her children, then she deserved to have the authorities called in.

"I'm hungry," Ollie said, hopping from the table to the bench and then the ground. "Momma said if we asked nice, you might give us some supper."

"You don't have to feed us," Karen interjected. "I made us sandwiches."

Ollie started to whine. "But I don't like—"

"Hush. She might let us spend the weekend if she doesn't have to feed us."

Dana felt more emotion pulse through her in sixty seconds than she'd allowed in the past five years. She'd chosen this job in the middle of nowhere to avoid feeling anything. Now white, scalding anger was directed at Beverly Moore, wherever she was. How dare she abandon her children as if they were overgrown vegetables easily left on the doorstep of unwary neighbors. But the tearstains on Karen's face had her fighting for control.

"I don't mind feeding you. Then I'll call some nice people to give you a place to stay." She tried to smile, but her face felt like it was cracking in half.

FRIDAY NIGHT was generally busy, but tonight, Brady Moore's usual rounds were quiet. He didn't know how many miles he'd driven that night along the county roads that wound from the Gabilan Mountains to the Diablo Range without seeing anything worrisome. No drunk drivers. No speeders. Always a bad sign. In his fifteen years as a sheriff's deputy for San Benito County, the quiet evenings were the ones that ended in something bad.

The dispatcher came over the radio. "There's a call from the Panoche School. Three juveniles abandoned."

"I'm in the south county," he replied. "Is there someone closer? Or maybe CPS?"

"You're going to want to take this one, Brady," the dispatcher said, her voice terse.

"Why?"

"Three girls," she emphasized. "Last name Moore."

Brady felt himself stiffen.

"Thought you might want to check it out before we call in CPS."

His brother Carson had three little girls whose last name was Moore.

Brady didn't carry around a lot of guilt. He didn't give a second thought to lying to drug dealers or unbalancing suspects, if it meant that he could clean up his little section of the universe. But it didn't take much soul-searching for him to realize that he'd been a bit too eager, nearly five years before, to oblige his sister-in-law when she'd told him to never contact her and the girls again.

Only fifteen months apart, he and his brother had grown up together, but even though Carson was older, he'd always been just a little too intellectual, too bookish to fit in well with his peers. That meant Brady had been the one who sold all of his brother's raffle tickets, fought his battles at school and introduced him to the world of girls.

It was no surprise when they grew up that they'd choose different career paths. Brady went into law enforcement, Carson into accounting. But the differences in their temperament only strengthened the bond between the brothers. Maybe that's why Brady had been so hurt when Carson had introduced him to his new wife, Beverly. Brady would never have dreamed Carson would give in to the impulse to marry a woman he'd only known twelve hours.

Even though Karen had been born ten months into their marriage, Bev hadn't seemed happy. But Carson's loyalty to his wife put an enormous amount of pressure on Brady and his mother, Edie, to accept her. And they'd tried. Since they'd left home, the brothers had always visited their mother once or twice a week. When Carson's visits dropped to once or twice a month, then eventually only on major holidays, it was hard for

Brady not to blame his sister-in-law. Especially once the reason for her unhappiness became clear.

Bev had thought Carson was a lot more successful than he actually was. Carson's accounting firm had a few good clients and was growing steadily, but the family lived on commissions and the small salary that Carson allowed himself, investing any other profit into the business or Karen's college fund. Bev wasn't content being a stay-at-home mom who needed to budget carefully. She wanted more—designer clothes for her and Karen. A nice car and house and furniture. She couldn't understand why Carson wouldn't move to the city and work in a big firm with big clients.

In spite of these differences, Brady believed Carson and Bev cared enough about each other to work out their problems. That was confirmed when the joyful pair announced they were expecting a second baby. Jean's birth was followed almost immediately by the conception of their third, and then all hell broke loose.

Edie—who'd never remarried after the death of her husband—had become sick and four terrible months later died. During those long days and endless nights of treatment and pain and sadness, Carson had managed only two short and awkward visits. In his grief, Brady's anger and resentment at his brother grew. It would have been nice if just once Brady could have relied on Carson. A month or two later, when Carson was arrested, Brady pretended not to care. His brother had completely changed. The irrefutable evidence showed this once honest and sensitive man had become an embezzler to further his wife's ambitions. Rather than help his brother through the complex legal system, Brady had turned his back. In what seemed to be just days, Carson accepted the court-appointed lawyer, took a plea and was sentenced to a minimum-security state penitentiary.

Bev, of course, blamed Brady, refusing to see how her own behavior had corrupted Carson. If it hadn't been for the girls, Brady would have gladly washed his hands of her. She wouldn't let him see the girls, so his only option was to deposit money directly into her account every month. It assured him that Bev wouldn't have to work and would maybe compensate for the fact that the children didn't have a father. It didn't help the guilt, though, and it didn't change the reality that his brother was a criminal. More than anything, it made Brady never want to get close enough to anyone to be that disappointed again.

"You still there?" the voice crackled over the radio.

"Yes."

"Are you going?"

"Yes."

"Should I notify CPS?"

No matter what had passed between him and his brother, no matter how much his sister-in-law hated him, he would not let the girls go into foster care. They were still his family.

"No," Brady said.

DANA TRIED TO GET through as much of her grading as she could. She spread the papers out before her on the table, feeling very anxious, while Karen, Jean and Ollie lay curled together on her couch. She adjusted her reading glasses and still squinted at the papers in front of her. She'd called the sheriff's department over an hour ago, but no one had come yet, though it was close to midnight.

Dana's chest tightened. The girls weren't trouble. Jean and Ollie had cried a little because they wanted to go home, but Karen had comforted them with adultlike pats and soft words, and they'd quickly settled down.

For their dinner, Dana had scraped together

three scrawny peanut butter sandwiches. She rooted through her kitchen cabinets looking for something that came from the fruit and vegetable portion of the food guide. She rose triumphant with a jar of peaches given to her by a parent. Laid out on the Corelle, the dinner didn't look too bad. Three pairs of large eyes, so stoic that a lesser woman would have wept, stood in the door of the kitchen, not even daring to enter.

"Dinner's on the table. Why don't you come in and eat?" she'd invited with a small smile.

"I'm not hungry, Miss Ritchie," Karen had said, her voice polite. She had her arms around her sisters. Ollie whispered something to Jean, who put her hand to Karen's ear. Karen listened and then looked up again. She reported, "But the girls are, so I guess they should eat. I don't need to."

"Come, all of you," Dana ushered them into the kitchen and got them seated. She should have put her arm around Karen and let her know that she didn't have to carry all that responsibility, and that everything was going to be all right. But Dana had done that before.

After the girls were settled and eating, Dana called her mother on the phone in her bedroom. "Have you called the police?" her mother had asked as soon as Dana had explained the day's events.

"Yes."

"Good." Her mother was emphatic. "I don't want you to get involved. Remember what happened last time."

Last time.

At first, her concern for the little kindergartener named Adam was strictly professional, then as the situation with his drug-addicted mother became clear, it turned to fond sympathy, followed quickly by a love she didn't believe she could feel for a child who wasn't hers. It changed her from a carefree young woman heedlessly taking an ordinary path from college to career to husband to children to fierce protector of the most innocent and underprivileged. No one could have predicted that all the love she'd had for Adam could vanish with one cold and ugly act. After that she'd changed again. This time into a woman who never wanted to be touched—emotionally or physically.

Her parents had stood by her the entire time, never questioning her decision to resign from her position at a progressive urban elementary school to sign on here. They'd simply helped her move. It was then that her mother—with a reassuring peck on the cheek—had warned her about hiding from her grief. But her mother had underestimated Dana's resolve. Dana was a smart, capable woman. If anyone could dodge grief, she would. She would conquer it by working so hard that her brain became numb.

One of the girls whimpered and Dana was brought back to the present. Karen, Jean and Ollie were fast asleep, their heads hanging at awkward angles. Dana looked at the stacks of papers in front of her, accepting the fact she wasn't going to get them done. She went over to the girls and straightened them out on the couch, placing a granny-square afghan over them. Adam had lain under this same blanket, giggling as he peered at her through the holes.

Karen opened her eyes. "Are they here yet?"

Dana shook her head. "Soon."

"Can't we stay here? This is comfortable." Her gray eyes were serious. "Momma said she'd be back on Sunday."

Dana couldn't keep them until Sunday. That was out of the question. They needed some motherly attention, a bath and clean clothes, real meals. Dana couldn't give them that.

"You'll be best off with people who can take care of you." Dana spoke in a practical tone. She knew where the conversation was leading as

Karen's lips pinched together to keep them from trembling. Jean moaned again.

"Is Jean okay?" Dana asked with concern. Before she could stop herself, she'd moved toward Jean and put a gentle hand on the small forehead.

"She's fine," Karen said quickly. "She has bad dreams sometimes."

Karen nudged her sister with her foot and Jean's eyes struggled to open. She was disoriented and her face crumpled with fear.

"It's just me, Jean," Dana soothed, the waves of some indefinable emotion washing through her. "You're okay."

Jean's face cleared and her eyes closed; clearly she'd never fully woken up.

"You can take us," Karen said, her voice small but brave.

Her back to Karen, Dana squeezed her eyes tight as she readjusted the afghan. "No, I can't. It's not right."

She ventured a look over her shoulder and felt even worse as Karen's eyes swam with tears. "Yes, it is. We get along okay at school, don't we?"

Dana couldn't answer that question, so she answered one that made her feel better. "A nice lady or man from Child Protective Services will come pick you up and find you a nice place to stay.''

''All of us? Together?'' Karen asked anxiously.

''I'm sure they'll try their best,'' Dana hedged and dropped her hands from the crocheted coverlet. She couldn't adjust the afghan forever.

''Why can't you keep us?'' Karen's clear treble had a pleading edge to it.

''I'm your teacher. Technically, I'm not even supposed to be baby-sitting you. And we need to know that you're okay if something happens to your mom.'' As soon as the words came out of Dana's mouth, she wanted to take them back. Karen, if possible, paled more.

''Do you think she's in trouble?''

This was another one of those situations in which a normal woman would tug the eleven-year-old into a tight hug and whisper heartfelt reassurances. Karen looked as if she would welcome that. Instead, Dana patted her arm. ''I'm sure she's okay. But it's good that you'll be with people who can take care of you. Try to get some sleep. They should be here soon.''

CHAPTER TWO

BRADY RAPPED on the door. He checked his watch and adjusted his belt, his heart beating erratically. Ridiculous. This wasn't a hostage situation; these were just little girls. Of course, it didn't help that he couldn't remember their faces or even the littlest one's name. Olive? Oleander? Would Bev actually name her daughter after a bush? He doubted that. Would he even know his nieces? They certainly wouldn't know him. He knocked again, automatically surveying the grounds. The school sat to the left of this small house.

"Just a minute," came the muffled response.

Brady looked at his watch again and stared at the front door. He heard rustling, then the door opened a crack and one eye peered at him. He noticed the flimsy chain on the door and the rotting wood it was clinging to. An intruder would have no difficulty entering this residence. A hefty shove would topple both the person attached to the eye and the door. Hardly safe for a woman living alone. He'd never met the schoolteacher but he didn't think that an elderly woman should be living out here all alone. He made a mental note to talk to her about safety.

She opened the door a little wider with a breath of relief. "Deputy…" She looked around him as if she was expecting someone else.

"Are you okay, ma'am?"

She nodded. "I'm just surprised."

"Surprised?"

"I thought that Child Protective Services would have at least sent a woman, since these are three young girls."

Brady swallowed, not wanting to lie to her. "I was sent out to evaluate the situation," he said instead. He wasn't sure who this was. Was she the schoolteacher's daughter? He couldn't stop staring at the freckles splattered across her nose as if someone had taken a paintbrush and flicked it at her. She couldn't be a day over thirty. Her plain T-shirt was tucked neatly into some well-fitting jeans, making her seem more youthful than she probably was.

She stepped back and gestured for him to come inside. "I am so glad you were able to get here on such short notice. I'm Dana Ritchie, Panoche School's teacher.''

Brady hid his surprise as he stepped through the doorway. ''You live alone, right?''

''Yes,'' she said abruptly. ''Is that a problem?''

Brady wondered what was making her so defensive. ''No. But you ought to get the door frame done in steel. And get a dead bolt and a peephole rather than that chain. You might want a dog for some additional protection.''

She blinked at him, a small smile coming to her lips. ''I'll talk to the school board about that on Monday. I'm not sure a dog is in my contract.''

Brady stepped farther into the foyer, pulling out his notebook. ''Now, what's the problem?''

She put her finger over her mouth, tilting her head in the direction of the living room. ''The girls are sleeping,'' she whispered. ''They've been waiting a long time.''

Brady swallowed. There was always a chance that these weren't his nieces.

''May I see them?'' he asked.

She nodded and quietly walked toward the couch.

Brady looked down at the sleeping girls. Their hair was falling over their faces, so he couldn't tell. Then the oldest girl's eyes popped open, wide and gray, guarded.

"Uncle Brady." It was a flat statement, surprising him. He didn't think Karen would recognize him. She'd only been seven when she'd last seen him.

"Karen."

"Uncle Brady?" the schoolteacher asked.

Brady stared at the woman who faced him, her head tilted, her eyes ready to do combat for these girls. "Brady Moore. I'm their uncle, their father's brother."

HE WAS THEIR UNCLE. These girls had family! Dana nodded and moved away, leaving Karen and the deputy watching each other. She was sure that he wasn't displeased by Karen, but he was glowering at the little girl. Surprisingly, Karen didn't blink. Her jaw tightened, but she never broke eye contact.

Quickly on the heels of the relief that came from learning the girls had family were second thoughts. How could Dana let these girls go off with a man who didn't even smile?

She glanced at Karen whose fingers poked through the holes of the afghan as she clutched it close to her. She didn't seem frightened, but neither was she reassured by the presence of her uncle. Dana took a deep breath and surprised herself by laying her hand on his arm.

"Deputy," Dana said to break the tension. He shifted his sharp gaze to her, and she tilted her chin to stare back. If Karen wasn't going to be intimidated, she wouldn't be either. She supposed he couldn't change the angles of his jaw to make him seem less authoritative or alter the keen intelligence in his eyes to make him appear less intense. She tried not to notice the flat crease of his pants. Meticulous. Not a hair out of place, not a little bit of five o'clock shadow.

On top of that, she noted with irritation, he was damn composed, given the situation he was in. Shouldn't he show just a smidge of embarrassment at his sister-in-law's behavior or some other kind of emotion that indicated this was a big deal? If Karen's reaction was any gauge, they weren't close. Yet Dana could feel him radiate a peculiar—for lack of a better word—detachment that she found more disturbing than his physical presence. His eyes swept over the room as if he was used to evaluating everything he saw.

She didn't know why a hot flush began to inch up her neck. She wasn't ashamed of her modest home. The furniture might not match, the rug was a brown, teal and purple throwback to the seventies, and the only decorations were student art projects from years before, but the place was clean and she liked it. So what if it screamed spinster schoolmarm.

He looked at her hand. "That grip is lethal."

Her face grew hotter when she realized she'd been clutching his arm. She abruptly dropped her hand and swung it behind her back.

"Maybe you should explain a few things," she suggested, glancing at the girls, all of whom were awake now.

Instead of responding, he watched the girls get off the couch and move over to Dana—who tried not to appear startled when Ollie's arm wrapped around her thigh.

"So, who do we have here?" he asked. Apparently, he realized that his glowering wasn't helping, because he crouched to give them a better look at him and kept his voice even and modulated. It sounded like a voice he used to calm, to hypnotize. Dana was impressed. She didn't want to be, but she was.

The same couldn't be said for the girls. They didn't say a word.

"I'm your Uncle Brady." He tried again with a smile, addressing Ollie but looking at Karen.

"I'm sure you don't remember me. You were just a baby when I last saw you. You sure have grown."

Silence.

"I guess your mom is gone?"

Dana had to give him points for trying. She prodded Karen, but the girl wasn't going to talk. Her gray eyes were huge as she sent Dana a silent plea to intercede.

"She went to a conference," Dana said, looking at Karen for confirmation.

Karen nodded and tugged on Dana's arm. "Miss Ritchie," she whispered.

"Yes, Karen?" Dana kept her voice low, though she knew Deputy Moore could hear every word they were saying.

"Don't let him take us." Her face had turned white.

"He's not going to hurt you, Karen. He's family." Dana's soothing words had the opposite effect on the girl. All the stoicism Karen had shown earlier was suddenly replaced with deep and uncontrollable sobs. Jean quickly started whimpering in sympathy.

The deputy looked at Dana for help, but she didn't know what to do.

"D-don't let h-him take us, Miss Ri-ritchie,"

Karen begged, her pleas coming out in an agonized rush. "We'll be good. We'll be so very good f-for you. We'll do everything you say and we'll help around the house. W-we won't be any trouble."

Biting her lip, Dana reached out a hand and gave Karen's shoulder an awkward pat. "Karen, I know this is a scary situation for you..." Even to her, her words were meaningless. When had she became so empty, so devoid of compassion that she couldn't gather a scared child into her arms and comfort her? Dana felt as if she had a dry piece of bread stuck in her throat. This was how it started. It only took one hug to open a heart. No matter how much Dana wanted to make this situation right, she couldn't.

She backed away, feeling as alone as Karen looked. She whispered into Ollie's ear. "I think Karen really needs a hug from you and Jean, don't you?"

Ollie let go of Dana's leg and flung her short arms around her older sister. Jean followed suit and together, the three girls sobbed.

"Can you keep them tonight?" a voice asked, low in her ear. She hadn't even seen him move, but he was right next to her and Dana felt her face flush under his steady scrutiny.

What a cold woman he must think she was. She turned away from him, not too numb to feel a tremendous amount of regret about that. She crossed her arms and pressed them closely to her chest to keep control of any feelings that threatened to erupt from within.

"I think they've been through enough," he continued, just for her to hear.

Dana could only nod as those unwanted emotions easily made their way through her barriers.

"*You've* been through a lot as well," he observed.

"I'm fine." Dana made her tone brisk and stepped away from him. She straightened her shoulders.

"You don't look fine."

"I'm fine," she repeated. "When you know me better, you'll realize I look like this all the time."

BRADY STARED at the woman in front of him, her body so stiff that it seemed as if she would shatter with the smallest of impacts. No one could look this way all the time. Her jaw was rigid. Her face was pale, her hands clenched into fists that hardened the muscles on her forearms. It seemed to take everything out of her to simply nod.

"It's pretty late," Brady said, projecting his voice in order to be heard over the crying. "I think it's better if we found a place for the girls to sleep here. What do you think, Miss Ritchie?"

"Yes." The demons she was fighting were gone, and she was back to business. She reached out to the children. "You'll be fine here tonight."

Brady watched the schoolteacher stretch tentative fingers toward Karen's hair. Her hand trembled as if she was afraid she would be burned from the contact. To help her, Brady knelt next to Ollie and put gentle hands on her tiny shoulders. She looked up, tears still in her eyes, but she wasn't afraid of him.

"I'll show you where the spare bedroom is," the schoolteacher said.

Ollie shook her head and hung on to Karen tighter.

With ease, Brady extracted the youngest girl from the trio and lifted her up.

"Oooh!" Ollie exclaimed with a delighted smile.

"Let go of her!" Karen jumped up, trying to grab Ollie. "You're not taking her anywhere."

"It's late," Miss Ritchie said. "Your uncle is just taking Ollie to bed."

Karen stopped jumping, uncertain. "Bed? Here?"

"Yes. Where you should have been hours ago."

"So does that mean we're not going with him?"

Brady tried not to feel stung by the relief in Karen's tone.

"For now. It's too late for you to go with your uncle. Your mom may make it back by tomorrow. So it's probably better for you to be here tonight."

Karen looked relieved and then turned to Brady with her arms open. "Give her to me. We can put ourselves to bed," she said. After he complied, Jean held on to the back of Karen's shirt, and the trio made their way down the hall. Ollie looked back over her sister's shoulder at him.

"G'night." She gave him a small wave with her fingers.

"Good night. I'll see you in the morning," he promised.

Karen turned in front of a bedroom door. "That's okay. We'll be fine. You don't have to come back." With that announcement, she and her sisters went into the room, Miss Ritchie behind them.

While he waited, he called dispatch and let them know the situation was taken care of, but that he would be at the residence for a while gathering information. He looked at his watch. He only had two hours left on this shift. The call complete, he took a more careful look at the small house. He studied the walls that were filled with a variety of construction-paper artwork. Lopsided snowmen shared equal space with tissue-paper mosaics. In the corner, there was a neat stack of egg and milk cartons. There was also a full box of cans stripped of their labels. He wouldn't have to be told that a teacher lived in this house.

He heard a sound behind him and turned to find the schoolteacher standing in the doorway. Her hands were behind her back and she stared at him with those dark eyes of hers. There was a pain in them that he couldn't understand and, for some reason, wanted to. He'd noticed there was no ring on her finger and remembered that the girls called her ''Miss Ritchie.'' Why was such a young woman holed up in such an isolated place?

She seemed to be waiting for him to say something, so he cleared his throat. ''Well, thank you.'' It didn't hurt to start with a thank-you.

''I can't keep the girls.'' The words were surprising in their bluntness.

Before he could discover what had motivated her to say them, Brady had to know what had happened to Bev. "Do you mind going through how the girls happened to be in your care in the first place?"

"Would you like some coffee?" she asked, obviously realizing this wasn't going to be a quick process.

"Yes," Brady answered easily. The task would give her something to do. Then she might relax enough to give him the kind of information he needed.

Brady watched her measure the coffee and put it into a filter, her movements careful and precise. He tried not to smile when she pulled from the cupboard the smallest coffeemaker he'd ever seen. He could down that much coffee at breakfast alone. She obviously wasn't addicted. She glanced up and their eyes met just for a split second. Brady swallowed hard. For a complete stranger, this schoolteacher had the oddest way of looking right through him.

She hurriedly plugged the coffeemaker into the wall before walking from behind the counter. "Why don't you sit down," she offered as she pointed to the table that separated the kitchen from the living room. "The coffee will only take a few minutes."

Brady sat, and she joined him, placing her forearms on the wooden table. She looked ready to answer questions.

"Why don't you tell me what happened?" He made his voice as friendly and conversational as he could. The tone worked, because he could sense that she relaxed a little once she realized he wasn't going to grill her.

She said, her words stark, "Their mother came by after school today and told me she didn't have a baby-sitter. She had to attend a conference this weekend and asked me to look after the girls. I told her no."

"Is that something you did often for Bev?"

She shook her head. "Never. I don't baby-sit my students. I have them from seven forty-five to two-thirty. That's all. No other parent has ever asked me to."

"But you have the children." He sat straighter. He could see a thin shield of defensiveness creep over her.

"Yes."

"So why don't you tell me how you came to take care of the children?"

The question was straightforward enough, but

the schoolteacher took a long time to answer. "I found them."

Brady felt a chill run down his spine. "Where?"

"Sitting on the picnic table." Her arm gestured in the general direction of the schoolhouse. "I didn't finish working until nearly nine o'clock."

"On a Friday?" he asked skeptically.

She flushed. "I have a lot of work to do. I'm not just the teacher. I'm the principal, too. I've got a ton of forms to fill out."

"No offense," he apologized hastily. "I just thought an attractive woman like yourself would have plans on a Friday night."

Her lips twisted into a wry smile. "There's not a lot of action around here after hours. What man in his right mind would drive an hour for a date with a woman who spends her day talking to children?"

Brady would consider it. If those eyes asked him, he'd consider doing almost anything for her.

"The children were sitting out there, waiting for me," she continued. "Thank goodness, it's a fairly warm night and that it was me. There's not a lot of traffic, but those girls were unsupervised for several hours. Anything could have happened to them."

DANA CLOSED HER EYES as the realization struck her. Anything. Anything could have happened to them and she wouldn't have known. Some stranger could have abducted them while they waited for her. Guilt pulsed through her.

"That isn't your fault," the deputy said.

She lifted her eyes to his as she felt slapped by terrible images from the evening news. There was no censure in his face, just empathy.

He continued on in that deep, rumbling voice. "Anything else?"

She didn't want to like talking to him. She didn't want to like the fact that this strange man at her kitchen table made her more comfortable than anyone else she'd met since coming to teach here.

She started to feel sick. She'd been awake too long and she desperately needed sleep, but she was so keyed up that she knew she wouldn't be able to. She swallowed, pressing her hands together so hard she saw the veins pop out on her forearms. She told herself to relax, but then jumped out of her chair to pour the coffee.

"Cream or sugar?" she asked.

"No."

"That's easy," Dana commented. She held out the cup.

He wrapped his large hand around it and her

hand as well. The cup nearly disappeared in his palm and her fingers felt engulfed by his. Dana couldn't stop looking at his hand, the unyielding, tanned skin and the prominent veins that traveled up his forearm to disappear in the dark hair. She tugged her hand away and sat down, pushing the chair back a foot or two to give herself some breathing room. Suddenly, it was very hot in the house.

"Any idea whether she would go north or south?" His eyes were fixed on her forearms. A small crease appeared between his eyebrows, but his expression remained pleasant.

Dana ran her tongue over her teeth. "I don't think you understand. I don't know enough about Mrs. Moore to really know where she went. I'm not sure anymore if it *was* a conference she had to attend. Maybe it was a meeting."

"Do you remember what Bev was wearing?" He wasn't writing, but Dana was certain that he would remember every word.

Dana looked at him in surprise. "Yes."

"Good." Dana's heart thumped as he flashed an even set of teeth at her. He prompted her again, "What was she wearing?"

Dana tried to remember and spoke slowly. "A

really nice suit. She had high heels and perfume on. Lots of makeup.''

"Do you know the color of the suit?''

"Taupe.''

"Taupe?''

"Taupe linen, with a cream silk camisole.''

"Oh.'' His expression was puzzled.

"Taupe's like a khaki brown without the green. Tan, with more gray,'' she explained.

"Anything else?''

The pause extended for much longer than she expected. He was giving her time to think, but she was only drawing a blank. She wasn't a very good witness. "I can't think of anything.''

"Are you sure?''

"Except for the occasional parent interviews, I don't speak to Mrs. Moore beyond hello, how are you.'' Dana stood up, feeling agitated, and then, realizing that her behavior was rude, sat right back down and clasped her hands together.

"I thought this was a small school.''

"What does that have to do with it?'' She was starting to get irritated, as if he held her responsible for his sister-in-law's disappearance.

"I thought at smaller schools pretty much everyone knew everyone else's business. The schoolteacher especially.''

She felt her back stiffen. "I am not a gossip." She was beyond irritated. She unclenched her hands and noticed bright red marks on her hands. She crossed her arms.

"I'm not asking for gossip. I'm asking for anything about Bev that could give us some insight into where she might have gone. Would you say that she was a devoted mother?"

Dana had to admire the finesse with which he spoke. Anyone could have been missing by the tone of his voice. Not a close family member. She cleared her throat. "Um, do you want the truth or the politically correct answer?"

BRADY STARED at the schoolteacher. She was alternately vulnerable yet fierce. Compassionate yet so reserved. However, it was the troubled look in her eyes that disturbed him the most.

"What's the difference?" he asked, making his tone light enough to match her dry one.

"The politically correct answer would be that she allows her children to be very independent."

"And the truth?"

"She forgets them. They're here really early and are always the last ones to get picked up. I've had to take them home a couple of times, when I wasn't able to get Mrs. Moore on the phone..."

Her voice trailed off and she avoided making eye contact, telling him she thought she'd said too much.

"Is there more?"

Dana studied her nails for a moment before answering. "No."

"Are you sure?" There was something in her voice that made him press her.

"Yes."

Brady waited. He knew there was more, probably more than she wanted to articulate. When another minute passed and she still hadn't spoken, he braced himself. This wasn't a good sign.

Finally she said carefully, her eyes still on her hands, each word precise, "The children are neglected. I can't prove it, but there's something about them that makes me think their home life is less than secure." She looked up at him. "Their clothes aren't clean. They aren't clean. They look neat, but they're not clean. I don't have anything to support my feelings, though I'm sure that if I were to put them in the tub, it'd be the first bath they'd had in a long time."

Brady didn't want to hear this. He didn't want to know that Carson's little girls were neglected. He felt a familiar stab of guilt that he'd used layers of rationalizations to dull. It didn't hurt any less.

"Do you think Mrs. Moore has abandoned them?" Dana asked, leaning forward. Her dark eyes were intense and Brady felt as if they saw into the deepest, ugliest part of him. He looked away. She couldn't know. Besides, she had her own secrets. Who was she to probe?

But he had to tell her something. How much?

She continued, "I don't know anything about their father. Out of state?"

He was embarrassed for Bev, for the girls, for himself. Bev had made it abundantly clear that when Carson "left her," as she put it, she didn't want anything more to do with his family. But knowing that didn't stop him from taking this personally. If Dana Ritchie was right about the girls being neglected, he was responsible.

"My brother is in prison." The words came out more bluntly than he intended. This schoolteacher was the first person who'd ever heard him utter those words, and he felt shame course through his body. Brady wasn't his brother's keeper, but he should have helped Carson more.

Dana didn't blink. "Oh."

He emptied the coffee cup and studied the pattern on it. Apples.

"That explains some things about the children. How long has he been in prison?" Her voice was matter-of-fact. She didn't react with the horror that he expected.

IT TOOK SO LONG for the man sitting across from her to answer that Dana began to wonder if he ever would. But she knew she had to be patient. This clearly wasn't easy for him.

"Since before Ollie was born." The words came out slowly and distinctly.

Dana studied his face. His mouth was tight but his hands encircled the empty cup as gently as if it was china. He was a man who carried around a lot of pain. She wanted to tell him she knew exactly how he felt. If she couldn't do that, she should at least give him a firm, reassuring hug or even a pat on the shoulder.

Instead, she said, "I'm sorry."

The words seemed trite and for some reason, that made her feel worse. The poor girls. Their father was in prison, their mother gone. Their future was even shakier than Dana had imagined.

"Yeah, me, too." He smiled. Despite the even teeth, the crinkling eyes and the deep dimples, Dana didn't believe it for a second. He tucked the pain somewhere behind that smile. Somehow, she knew he worked just as hard as she did, so he wouldn't have to think about the past.

"Is that why you haven't seen the girls?" She leaned against the back of a chair. She chose her words with care, sending them out as an exploratory probe.

"Partly." He stood up and turned to stare at her wall of student art. "I've been busy."

Usually such a rebuff would make Dana back off, but for some reason, she said, "It must be hard to be in law enforcement and have a brother in prison."

She kept her voice soft. She'd found a kindred spirit in this man who kept as much hidden as she did.

"It happens." He strode across to the kitchen and put the coffee cup in the sink. Then, as if compelled, he rinsed it.

Dana didn't want to press, but needed to know one piece of information, "The girls' father, your brother, isn't in jail for hurting—" Her voice faltered. She couldn't bear the idea that those little girls had suffered in other ways, as well.

The *"No!"* exploded out of Brady, but his back was still toward her. He took a deep breath and then turned around. His mask was on again and his voice reasonable when he spoke. "No. He's

not in jail for any kind of violent crime. It's—"
He didn't finish.

Dana didn't blame him. She could feel how tired he was, and her own fatigue responded to it. "I'm sorry, I didn't mean—"

He shook his head and waved a hand. He pushed himself away from the counter, the smile back on his face. "It's not your fault. You haven't done anything. In fact, I should be thanking you for all that you've done for the girls."

"So what happens now?" Dana asked.

"What happens is that I let you go to sleep and I'll come back in the morning. Maybe by then Bev will have found her way home."

Dana took a deep breath, relieved that he was planning to return. Having another person around would make this easier.

She stood and started to move toward the front door, pleasantries dying on her lips as a terrified scream came from the bedroom.

CHAPTER THREE

DANA TURNED at the screech of pure anguish coming from the girls' bedroom. She ran down the hall with Brady right behind her.

"What's wrong?" he asked her.

"I don't know."

He stepped in front of the door and rattled the knob. "It's locked."

"It can't be. There isn't a lock on it." Dana pushed Brady out of the way. "Karen! Open up." She shoved the door with her shoulder. "There's a chair or something against it."

"Karen, take the chair away from the door," Brady called.

"No. It's okay." Karen's voice trembled.

"It's not okay," Dana said in her best teacher voice. "You need to open this door. We need to see if anyone's hurt."

"No one's hurt," Karen said with a little more confidence. "You can go away. Sorry to bother you."

The screaming got louder.

"Who is that?" Brady asked Dana in an undertone.

She listened at the door, trying to figure out what was going on. She could hear Ollie making soothing sounds. "Jean," she concluded.

"Karen," Brady cajoled. "Open the door so Miss Ritchie can take care of Jean."

"It's okay." Karen's brave little voice came through the door. "Jean just had a bad dream, that's all."

"Let us in," Dana pleaded.

"It's okay," the girl repeated.

"It's not okay until I see Jean," Dana said. She turned to Brady, unfortunately finding him close enough for her face to brush against his chest. She looked down and asked, "So do you have a way of kicking in the door?"

"I'm not going to kick in the door." Brady was adamant.

She rattled the handle.

"Ollie," she called. "Take the chair away from the door."

"Don't do it!" Karen's order to Ollie was loud and clear.

"Maybe she can help Jean," Ollie said.

"No. She's just going to get into trouble." This was said so low that Dana had to strain to hear it.

"Ollie, let me in. No one's going to get into trouble. Honest," Dana coaxed.

"What's going on?" Brady asked in her ear. She could feel his breath on the back of her neck.

"They think they're going to get into trouble because Jean's screaming."

"She's *nice*," Ollie argued. Dana could tell that she'd moved next to the door.

"But *he's* out there." That was ominous.

"They're worried about you," Dana explained to Brady in a whisper.

"Me?"

Dana glanced up at him, surprised that he looked hurt. "You can't take it personally. You look, uh, intimidating—as if you're going to take them to jail."

He knocked on the door. "We both promise that no one will get into trouble." He had to shout, because the agonized screeches that had started to subside into heartbreaking whimpering were getting louder as Karen and Ollie argued.

"I'm going to open it," Ollie declared.

They heard a fumbling at the door and then it swung open. Jean—her face contorted with terror—was curled in the corner of the sofa bed that Dana had pulled out for the girls to share.

Karen tried to block their view of Jean. "She's going to be okay. If you have to put someone in the closet, then it should be me. You can't put Jean in the closet. She doesn't mean to have bad dreams."

Dana shook her head, wanting to believe there was some other reason that Karen had come to this conclusion. "Why would we want to put any of you in the closet?"

"That's what you do." Karen's arms were firmly planted on her skinny hips, leaving no one with any doubt that she would defend her sister to the last. The sight broke Dana's heart. No eleven-year-old should have to bear that much responsibility.

"*I* don't. I just want to see what's wrong with Miss Jean," Dana scooted around Karen and pulled the shrieking girl into her arms. Sitting on the bed, she nestled Jean on her lap and began to rock, resting her cheek on the child's grubby head.

JEAN CRIED HARDER as she huddled into the safety of the schoolteacher's arms. Brady couldn't remember ever feeling such anger before. In his fifteen years as a deputy sheriff, he'd seen a lot of horrible things, but the neglect and abuse of kids was the worst. True innocents at the mercy of the adults in their lives. If he thought about it enough, he would never go to work.

He made an effort to unclench his hands as he added Karen's words to the growing pile of evidence against Bev. Something would have to be done and done quickly. Child Protective Services was out of the question. There was no way he'd let the girls get taken and most likely separated. One member of the family institutionalized was enough. Besides, he owed it to Carson not to let these girls suffer anymore. Still worse—what if Bev *did* show up? Then he'd never be able to get the children into a decent home setting without involving CPS. He had to act before that happened. But what could he do? Even though he was their closest living relative and a deputy, that hardly testified to his fitness as a guardian. If he was married, with a family and a house, there wouldn't be a problem. The courts would give him custody in a flash. But the fact was he worked odd shifts and had a tiny studio apartment, not exactly the ideal situation for three young girls, even temporarily.

"Did you have a nightmare, sweetie? It's okay.

You're safe now." Dana's crooning broke into his thoughts. She was a natural mother... He immediately rejected the plan that began to form. *No. Ridiculous.*

Ollie put her hand on Dana's thigh and looked pleadingly at the schoolteacher, tears brimming in her eyes. "You're not going to put Jean in the closet, are you? You said you don't do that."

Dana shook her head. "My closets are for coats and school supplies. I don't think Jean would make a very good school supply, do you?"

Ollie looked puzzled. "What would she be?"

Dana frowned, thinking it over. Brady felt a curious emotion begin to spread through his chest, squeezing his heart like a giant hand. He couldn't stop watching the schoolteacher and the girls. Ollie's sweet face was filled with a grave earnestness that Dana apparently could not resist, because she reached out and gave the girl's plump cheek a reassuring rub. That gesture alone sealed things for Brady. He couldn't save these kids by himself, but together *they* could. They could provide a home for Karen, Jean and Ollie. The plan terrified him, even though it made perfect sense.

"Well," Dana said, answering Ollie's question with utter seriousness. "I think she'd be an awfully good paper clip."

A little laugh burst out of Ollie. "But she'd have to lie flat all the time."

"Could she be a staple?"

"No! Scissors!" Ollie chortled and made a big cutting gesture with her arms.

"She'd have to snip things," Dana reminded her.

Brady watched in bemusement as Jean's wails subsided to occasional hiccups. Even though she didn't say anything, the brightness in her eyes indicated she was listening.

"I know," Dana told Ollie, giving Jean another squeeze. "Jean could be the paste!"

"She'd have to be really, really, really sticky," Ollie said, bouncing up and down on the bed. Then she froze and Brady saw a wet stain start to spread across the sheet. Ollie's face collapsed and her tears returned. "I didn't mean to."

"What's wrong, honey?" Dana asked.

Ollie didn't say a word, but the tears spilled onto her cheeks.

"I think she's had an accident." Brady gestured to the spreading stain.

"Oh." Dana didn't blink. She gave Ollie a big smile. "I think you need to go to the potty right now."

"No cl-cl-oset?" Ollie whimpered.

"You don't look like a Magic Marker to me. Go sit on the potty right now." With considerable effort, Dana managed to stand with Jean in her arms, then she moved over to Brady and thrust the girl at him. His surprise must have shown. Dana grinned at him. "It's either Jean or potty duty. Your choice."

It really wasn't that crazy a plan. "I'll take Jean," he said, pulling the child close to his chest and being careful not to poke her with the edge of his badge.

Dana nodded as she left the room with Ollie. "I thought you might."

Brady thought Jean had fallen asleep she was so quiet and still, but when he looked, her huge eyes were peering up at him.

"She thinks you're going to put her in the closet," Karen informed him.

"Why would she think that?" Brady made his voice neutral so Karen wouldn't detect his anger.

"That's where Momma puts us when we're bad."

Brady felt a chill run down his spine. "Your mother shouldn't do that."

Karen shrugged. "We always deserve it, and anyway it's only for a little while. Just a day or so. She's always nice when she lets us out."

Brady didn't want to hear any more. He sat on the bed and turned his gaze to Jean who was tracing the ridges on the seal of his badge with her small index finger. Then, in a move of complete trust, she snuggled closer into him, the sharp bones of her elbows jabbing into his ribs.

He sat that way for what seemed like a long time and analyzed his plan from all angles. If he tried to file for temporary custody on his own and didn't get it, there would be only two places for the children to go—back to Bev, if and when she returned, or into the system. Neither option was acceptable.

Bev would probably move out of the area, and the poor girls would just be treated like excess baggage until she deserted them again or, worse, found a more permanent way of ridding herself of her children.

In Child Protective Services, the girls might go to a good home, but then again they might not. The likelihood that they'd be split up would be high. Ollie and Jean had good chances to be adopted, but Karen was too old. Crazy as the plan had seemed ten minutes ago, by the time Dana returned to the room with Ollie wrapped in a towel, her cheeks scrubbed to a bright pink, Brady knew the only way to ensure that he would be granted temporary custody of the children by the judge would be if he were to get married. And since there was no woman in his life—certainly no woman the girls would trust—that meant he had to convince Dana to be his bride.

"Sorry it took so long," Dana apologized. "It was just easier to give her a bath." She produced three folded T-shirts. "Nightgowns," she announced, quickly pulling one over Ollie's head. She handed another to Karen.

"Now, who wants to help me change the sheets?" she said, her voice bright, obviously unaware that while she, Ollie and Karen worked, he was finalizing his plan. It made perfect sense. Not all marriages started with love. She seemed to be a pleasant enough woman and practical, too. Being a schoolteacher in such a rural area proved her dedication to children. He didn't doubt that he'd grow to love her, in, of course, a brotherly way—over time.

"I think a bath is in order for Miss Jean," Dana said once the bed was remade. "When I feel sad, a warm bath always makes me feel better. Also, monsters don't like water."

"Another bath?" Brady asked.

Dana gave him a small smile that caused a

pulse to beat erratically in his throat as she held out her arms for Jean. "Come on, missy."

Okay, not so brotherly.

"I like baths," Ollie said sleepily, already snuggled down into the clean sheets. "You make them fun."

"Thank you, miss. Now, you have a good night's sleep." Dana dropped a kiss on Ollie's cheek. "For Miss Jean, we are going to have a special keep-the-meanies-away kind of bath."

"I can do it," Karen said.

Dana looked gently at Karen, "You've done so much already, I think you should rest, because you're going to have to be strong for tomorrow."

"Still—" Karen shrugged "—I usually do it."

"I promise to take good care of her," Dana offered. "Do you mind? I like giving little girls baths."

Karen looked undecided and then crawled into bed next to Ollie. She ignored Brady and addressed Dana. "He's leaving, right?"

Dana communicated three different messages with one meaningful glance at Brady.

"Uh, yes." He started to walk out of the room. "I'll be back tomorrow."

Karen didn't look pleased, but finally nodded. "I guess that's okay."

It was a halfhearted endorsement, but Brady felt as if it was a gift.

DANA RAN a warm bath for Jean, peeling off the filthy pajamas that Dana had reluctantly allowed them to put on earlier. Calm now, Jean happily put her hand on Dana's shoulder and stepped into the tub.

"Let's do your hair first. I'm going to put some warm water on it, so close your eyes really tight," Dana said, her voice soft.

Jean shut her eyes, her face scrunching up with the effort, and Dana poured warm water onto the matted mess. She definitely wasn't wrong about the children's lack of hygiene. Only after three washes did Dana feel the little girl's hair was clean. She was thankful there weren't any lice.

"Can you wash yourself, Jean?" Dana asked, offering her a bright-orange bath puff.

Jean nodded, took the puff and lathered it up. With earnest determination, she scrubbed her arms, chest and legs. When she finished, she looked up at Dana, who finished off the little girl's face, neck and back. She was relieved when she didn't see any marks or bruises anywhere.

"There!" Dana said when she'd finished rinsing the soap off. "The monsters wouldn't dream of eating such a clean little girl. They hate the taste of soap."

Jean gave her a ghost of a smile and stepped right into the towel Dana held open for her. Dana closed her eyes and felt a lump in her chest. She swallowed hard. She didn't want to feel anything for this child. But her heart wasn't as atrophied as she'd always thought.

Jean patted her face, her little forehead furrowed with concern.

Dana blinked back tears. "I'm fine. You're just so cute."

Jean shook her head and wrapped her arms around Dana's neck. Forcing herself not to reject the kindness Jean offered, she squeezed back, then stood. "Oh, you're so heavy!"

After she combed out Jean's hair, she carried the girl to the bedroom, where Ollie slept and Karen had her eyes shut. Shortly, Jean was in a T-shirt, tucked in next to her sisters.

Before she left, Dana pushed back Karen's hair and kissed her forehead. Then she whispered "Sleep well" in her ear. As she turned off the light, Karen spoke.

"Miss Ritchie?"

"Yes, Karen?"

"What's going to happen to us?"

"I don't know. But everything will work out in the end."

"Promise?"

Dana swallowed. "Yes. I promise."

Karen nodded and pulled the covers over her head as she nestled closer to Ollie.

Dana crept from their room and closed the door, but she could get no farther. She leaned up against the wall, trying to hold back the emotions that surged through her. She couldn't do this again. Already, she liked these little girls more than she should. She didn't want to care for them only to have them ripped away. She'd done that once before. In his two months with her, Adam had gone from an introverted six-year-old to a brave and joyful boy. Then—

No. She wouldn't think of that anymore. She stood straight and headed for the kitchen. These three girls were Deputy Moore's problem, not hers.

He was sitting at the table, but got up when she entered. "Miss Ritchie."

"Dana." She smiled, feeling the fatigue all the way down to her toes. "I think that we know each other well enough now to use first names. Unless that's against policy or something."

He shook his head and pulled a chair out for

her, a gesture she found oddly touching. Then he
sat down and reached across the table to close his
fingers over hers.

"Thank you." His voice was grave.

"For what?" His warm touch was doing something odd to her breathing. He looked different,
too. Something about him had changed in the
short time he'd been here.

"For what you've done for these children," he
answered.

She dismissed his thanks with a shrug. "For
being a decent human being?"

"For being a caring human being. I couldn't
have done what you did tonight."

"Night terrors. It's common for children."
Suddenly, Adam's face loomed in front of her
eyes. She tried to tug her hand away from
Brady's, but he hung on.

"Thank you," he said again, stressing the
words. "I *owe* you."

It was a plain statement, but oddly intimate and
filled with emotion. Dana shook her head, almost
recoiling from the thought of Brady Moore being
in her debt. She could hardly bear to have Jean,
sweet-smelling and damp from her bath, touch
her. She couldn't imagine how difficult it would
be to see Karen's rumpled morning hair, the sleep

in the corners of Jean's eyes, the creases left by the pillowcase on Ollie's cheek. She could protect her heart from those things. But what would protect her from this man's gratitude?

AS DANA SQUIRMED, clearly discomfited by his appreciation, Brady's throat constricted. She had no idea the front of her T-shirt was plastered to her. It revealed no more than the outline of her bra and soft curves, but her indifference to her appearance was appealing. He didn't know what scared him most—the thought she'd say no or yes. He would understand her reasons for saying no. There were a hundred reasons for it, none more compelling than the fact they'd only known each other a couple of hours. Although he had to admit that the intensity of their time together made him feel as if he knew Dana better than some women he'd dated for several months. Still, she was going to think he was crazy.

"Looks as if you took a bath, too," he commented.

She grinned and inhaled deeply. Brady could actually see her relax.

"We need to talk," Brady plunged on with the conversation he'd been having with himself.

"That sounds very serious."

"It is. It concerns you and the girls. And me." He paused. "They seem to be very comfortable with you."

"I know them from school."

He nodded. "Their situation is pretty bad. And I was hoping that we could find a way between us to keep the girls."

KEEP THE GIRLS? Dana's mind spun in several directions at once. Brady continued to talk, but she couldn't hear him. *Keep the girls.* She'd had Adam for two months. It had taken one week to fall in love with him and five years to grieve his death. What would caring for Karen, Jean and Ollie do to her?

"There must be appropriate foster homes." Her voice sounded weak to her own ears.

"Take it from me. There are very few of those. The number of needy children far outpaces the homes available. More than likely, they'll end up in a holding facility until they can be placed." Brady's voice was clinical. "The good ones are filled and some are highly questionable. It's just income for some folks."

When Dana didn't say anything, Brady continued, "Social services would more than likely split up the girls, and I think that's going to unsettle them even more. Especially Karen. You can see that she considers her sisters her responsibility. If they were taken from her, she might never recover.''

''They're not my concern.'' Dana couldn't help how harsh the words sounded. But she refused to feel guilty. She wasn't going to endure another loss. She wasn't going to grieve for the Moore girls if something went wrong. Her mind was screaming, but she sat quietly as Brady got up to pace in the small living room.

Brady's sober tone broke the silence. ''Dana, it's true that the girls aren't your concern. I know you were forced to take them. But I also know that without you, the girls aren't going to have much of a future.''

''Why?'' She didn't want to hear this. She could tell he was a meticulous man, one who wouldn't do things on a whim. While she'd been bathing Jean, he'd sat at her kitchen table working out his plan to have the girls move in with her.

Brady knelt in front of her. ''Have you thought about what would happen if their mother came back tomorrow?''

Dana felt as if he'd sucker punched her. She shook her head. ''Frankly, I haven't been thinking about anything except what's happening right now."

"I understand. But all I've been thinking about is that damn closet and how much I don't want Bev to have these girls anymore."

"But she's their mother. There's not a lot of evidence of abuse." She heard the denial in her tone, knew it was wrong. But had to try to protect herself.

"There's been enough," he said. "One way to help the girls is to call CPS."

"Which I tried to do tonight, but got you instead."

He gave her a disarming smile, his first real one. "You may not be so glad about that, but I know it was a gift. Dana, if CPS gets involved, it will mean automatic foster care until the situation is worked out."

"But you're their uncle. Surely the state would see that you can provide them a good home," Dana protested. "As next of kin, their care would revert to you, right?"

"Not necessarily," Brady said. "Once this becomes an official situation, I would have to undergo a home study. I can tell you right now I wouldn't pass. I live in a studio apartment with a pull-out couch. And I work shifts—hardly an ideal environment for three little girls. That means the girls would be in foster homes until I got everything together to pass the home study."

"Is there another way?" Dana asked, knowing the answer was going to involve her.

Brady inhaled and clasped her left hand in both of his. The warmth traveled up her arm. "Yes. We get married, hire a lawyer and file for temporary custody with the county. There are a few people who owe me favors. Once they understand the circumstances, they'll help push this through the system."

"Excuse me?" Dana blinked. He was definitely crazy. She'd expected him to suggest moving the girls in with her, but he was talking about something entirely different.

"I know quite a few people who would help us do this," he repeated.

"No. No." Her free hand fluttered through the air. "Back up a little more."

"We'd file for temporary custody."

She shook her head. "No, before that."

"Hire a lawyer?"

"No, before that."

"Oh, getting married. I know it sounds crazy,

especially since we've only known each other a few hours, but we *do* make a good team.''

"You did say *married*.''

"If we were married, there would be no judge that wouldn't grant us temporary custody, especially if you testify to the abandonment.''

"And temporary custody means what?'' Dana was feeling faint. Eight hours ago, she'd refused to baby-sit these girls. Now she was being proposed to by a man she hadn't known existed before midnight. She wouldn't do it. She couldn't do it.

She could teach them to read and write, put Band-Aids on their skinned knees, praise them when they mastered long division, but she couldn't let them stay at her house, filling it up with their sweetness and laughter, any more than they already had. "What does temporary custody mean?'' she repeated.

Brady's eyes were sympathetic, as if he could tell what she was thinking. But he couldn't. How could he when he didn't know about Adam? "Temporary custody means that even if Bev comes back, she can't get the kids until *she* files with the court. That means the burden is on her to prove that she's a good mother.''

"And when did you get this brilliant idea?"

Brady was silent and then said honestly, "Since you held Jean in your lap." Brady squeezed her hand and continued, "It wouldn't have to be a real marriage, obviously, just one that can get me custody of the kids. Once I have time to work out a new work schedule and find another place to stay, we can get the marriage annulled."

"Annulled?" Dana felt like he'd sprayed her with cold water, then frowned at her reaction. An annulment made perfect sense. It wasn't as if they could have a real marriage or make a real family. This was just to protect the girls.

"Yes, annulled. That way you can be free to marry whomever you want later without any legal complications."

"And what's in this for me?" She felt her voice rise an octave.

"I don't have a lot of money, but I can compensate you for your time and effort."

Dana was sure Brady never saw the hand that whacked him squarely across the top of his head. She wasn't even sure why she'd whacked him.

"What? I'm sorry. What did I say?"

"*Compensate me?*" Dana was angry at the

whole situation. She was fuming, boiling mad. "Give me money? What am I—a rent-a-wife?"

"Well, no, I wasn't thinking about it quite in that way," he muttered and rubbed the side of his head. "You need to be careful. You pack a wallop."

Dana sat back in her chair. "I'm not sorry."

"What did you want me to say? You've already gone far beyond the duty of any concerned citizen. You've opened your house to us. You've been generous with your time and your attention. You don't think that deserves some kind of compensation?"

She tilted her chin. "Okay. What's the going rate for a wife?"

"I don't know. I haven't calculated it yet. Maybe we can work it out in terms of days. Ow!" He rubbed the top of his head where she'd smacked him again.

"Why didn't you just lie and say that it's about keeping those girls in a happy household?" she asked.

"It's about that, too," he said. "And that's not a lie. I wouldn't even think of asking you if I didn't think this would work out for everyone."

Dana kept silent as Brady writhed in misery.

Finally, she asked, "Compensation aside, when were you thinking about doing this?"

"Sunday."

"As in tomorrow?" Her voice squeaked.

"I want custody before Bev gets back from her conference."

"And filing for custody?"

"We can do it at the same time. Get married and file for custody. We can pick up a lawyer on the way to the courthouse."

"The courts aren't open on weekends, especially not on a Sunday," she pointed out.

"They can be."

"Don't these things take time?"

"I'll set it up. I know a lot of people."

She didn't doubt it. He'd probably already made a list of the people he needed to call.

"Can I have time to think about it?"

"Yes."

"Do I get a ring?" It was ironic really. Negotiating for a ring. She didn't even know why she was doing it. Except that it might make this all seem like less of a lie.

"If that will make you say yes, then you can have a dozen rings."

"Okay. I'll think about it," she promised. She

didn't want to be rude, but she'd had just about all she could take of Brady Moore. Maybe in the daylight, he would see that his proposal was more than absurd. "Don't you have to leave now? Write up a report?"

He took her cue and stood. "I'll come back after breakfast."

Dana glanced meaningfully at the clock. "You mean in a few hours."

He smiled. "I'll try to give you time to sleep in."

"It doesn't matter. Even if you do, I'll be up with the kids."

"Later. We'll talk about it more later." He walked to the front door and stopped to study the chain on her door.

Dana followed him, puzzled. What was he looking at?

"I'll fix that, too," he added absently, before turning back to her. She couldn't define the emotion in his eyes, but the force of it slammed into her. She backed up a step and looked down.

Dana swallowed hard. Then she glanced up, but he'd shuttered the emotion so quickly, she wasn't sure she'd seen anything. She was tired, that's all.

She'd had a draining night and it was several hours past her bedtime.

"Dana," he said.

"Yes?"

"If you say no, I'll understand. You've already done more than enough for my family. It is a crazy idea."

She just nodded and watched him get in his patrol car. Yes, it was a crazy idea. So why was she considering it?

CHAPTER FOUR

AT NOON, SATURDAY, Dana and the girls waited in front of Beverly Moore's house for Brady, who had called earlier and asked her to meet him there. That way the girls could collect some of their belongings to feel "more at home." He hadn't pressed her for her answer, but as her heart pounded, he'd told her everything he was planning to do to file for temporary custody. For a man who'd promised to give her time to think, Brady was acting an awful lot like her acceptance was inevitable.

Perhaps it was.

He's a stranger, her mind had chided after she'd hung up the phone and hopped out of bed to feed the girls breakfast. She'd only had plain cereal and brown toast but all three girls had eaten every little bit without complaint. In fact, Ollie had eaten as if it was the first meal she'd had in days. Partly in amusement, but mostly in horror, Dana had watched the little girl stuff two pieces of toast into her mouth until her cheeks puffed out like a chipmunk's. No matter how many reassurances Dana made, Ollie could not seem to stop gorging on food.

Now, Dana and Karen watched Jean and Ollie play tag on what could only be called a front lawn by a most generous person. Dana tried not to be judgmental of the weeds that were so tall that they almost obscured the two young girls, or the windows so thick with grime that it was impossible to see inside, because she knew how sensitive Karen was. Even though they'd only been here for a few minutes, the oldest girl was nervous and restive. She sat on the step far away from Dana, tapping her foot. Then, she jumped up to pace, then she sat down again.

"I thought you said Uncle Brady was going to meet us here." Karen's voice was accusing.

"He said he would meet us here at noon," Dana replied in as soothing a voice as she could muster. She knew how difficult this situation was for Karen, and she also knew that Karen wasn't yet fully prepared to trust her uncle.

"Well, what time is it?"

Dana held her watch up for Karen to see. "Noon."

"Then where is he? He's not going to come."

"He's going to come." Dana made her voice as firm and positive as she could.

"How do you know?"

"I trust him," Dana told Karen, surprised at her words. Since she was a loner by nature, it was incredible that this man had muscled his way into her inner circle, almost as if he belonged there. "If he said he was coming, he'll be here."

Dana knew what she said was true. Brady Moore had the kind of integrity that was unshakable, even under times of great conflict and stress. He'd made a promise. Nothing would keep him away.

Karen sighed and stood up again.

"Anything wrong?" Dana asked.

Silently Karen rocked from foot to foot, keeping her legs extended and straight. She looked like Gumby. Dana would have told her so, but the young girl spoke first. "My mom's maybe not the best housekeeper."

Dana laughed. "Who is, these days?"

"No. I really mean it." Karen's eyes were serious and she hesitated before saying, "You won't not like us if the house is a little messy, right? I'm in charge of cleaning it up."

Karen was truly troubled, and Dana felt a pang

of sympathy for the girl who had so much responsibility.

"I think there's very little that would make me not like you." Dana couldn't stop those words any more than she could stop Brady Moore from proposing.

Karen turned away from her, but continued to talk, "Sometimes Ollie is a real brat."

Dana resisted the urge to smile as she watched Ollie and Jean playing. "I won't hold Ollie's brattiness or a messy house against you," Dana assured her. "Honest. Come sit next to me." Dana ignored the warning signal in her head. First, Karen sat closer, and then the next thing Dana knew she was making room in her life for these poor little girls. As if that wasn't bad enough, these girls came with an uncle. Dana swallowed. She was afraid he would be the one she'd need to protect herself from the most.

After a brief hesitation, Karen settled down next to her, her small body pressing against Dana's side. Dana was surprised to find that she didn't dislike the contact. She even had to shut her eyes and fight the urge to put her arm around Karen's shoulders. Jean and Ollie, who'd been playing in the yard, stopped when they saw Karen sitting so close. Like magnets, they were drawn inexorably to any affection they sensed.

Dana barely had time to brace herself before they both hurled themselves into her lap. Uh-oh. This was exactly the behavior that would make her fall in love with them, make her say yes to a marriage proposal from a man she didn't know at all.

She took a deep breath.

"I got hurt," Jean said shyly, her little index finger poking Dana in the chest.

Dana exhaled, thankful for the distraction. "What happened?"

Jean pulled up her knee. On close inspection, Dana saw a very tiny scratch.

Dana touched it with gentle fingers. "How did you do that?"

Jean pointed to Ollie.

"I didn't do it. The ground did it." Ollie squirmed almost completely around to look up at Dana. "You're really pretty."

Dana knew the right thing for her to do was to pat Jean on the head and tell her to suck up the pain. And that was exactly what she planned on doing. But before she could stop herself, she'd leaned over and planted a feather-light kiss on

Jean's grubby knee. "There. Now it will feel better."

Jean beamed at her.

Ollie touched her face. "You're really pretty," she repeated.

Dana tapped her forefinger on Ollie's pert nose. "You are, too."

Karen leaped to her feet suddenly. "I think that's him." She pointed to the small speck in the distance.

"Are you sure?"

"Don't know. I'm going to go check." She ran full speed down the long, dirt driveway, Jean and Ollie only seconds behind her, all three finally stopping at the mailbox.

Dana settled back against the brick to wait. What was she supposed to do? Not kiss a boo-boo? Adam's image was so clear that Dana felt she could touch him. But he wasn't really there. He never would be again. She stood up and looked at her watch. The truck Karen had seen didn't turn into the driveway, but the girls weren't deterred. They whooped as they spotted another vehicle coming toward them.

Glancing at her watch, Dana tried not to doubt him. Living in the country meant allowing people the time to get from one place to another. But it was twelve-thirty. Should she leave a note and go home? How long were they supposed to wait?

Just as she'd made up her mind to leave, she heard screams and squeals. Sure enough, an old blue truck was turning into the driveway. She watched it stop at the mailbox. After a brief conversation with Brady, the three girls clambered into the truck bed. Dana frowned. That wasn't exactly safe. But then, she had to grin. Brady was driving slower than she would have thought possible. The girls whooped and cheered as the truck crawled forward. For the first time since their mom had dropped them off, they looked as carefree as little girls were supposed to.

It took a good ten minutes for the truck to reach the house. By that point Dana found herself with a stomach full of jitters. As Brady got out of the truck, she saw he was dressed in jeans with a light-blue chambray shirt, the sleeves rolled up to expose his forearms. Without his uniform, he was almost ordinary. *Almost.* When Dana caught his smile, she felt her own lips tug upward. There was nothing ordinary about those dimples or the intensity in his hazel eyes.

"I know, I'm late," Brady said before she could say anything. "It took me a lot longer to do everything I needed to."

Dana nodded, understanding his need for vagueness. She gestured to the door. "Let's go in."

Brady pulled out a device that she didn't think was legal.

"Can you buy those at the hardware store?" Dana whispered in his ear.

His oblique smile was her answer, but before he could use it, Karen stopped him.

"I have a key," the girl offered, her eyes lifting to his for approval.

"Even better." Brady smiled down at her. Karen averted her eyes, but Dana could tell the girl's suspicion of her uncle was waning. Both adults stepped back to let Karen insert the key into the lock and push the door open.

A terrible stench wafted out like a cloud of noxious gas. Undeterred by the sickening smell, the girls ran into the house.

"Stop!" Dana called in alarm, gasping at the overwhelming odor. When they paid no attention, she plunged into the house after them.

BRADY RECOILED, but entered the house a few moments after Dana. He easily found the light switch, but seeing the house clearly only seemed to make the stench worse. With an angry stride, he headed across the living room to tug open a window. Silverfish scurried along the sill. Disgusted, he worked his way around the perimeter of the room, opening every window. While his actions eased the smell slightly, they did nothing to ease his anger.

Dana stood in the middle of the room, the horror of what she was seeing naked on her face.

In his job, Brady had seen some awful places—crack houses filled with cigarette butts, spilled food and soiled diapers, metamphetamine labs where lethal chemicals were stored beside playpens, but this was worse. Maybe because he never would have expected his sister-in-law's house to look like this. Dammit! Bev had money. The automatic deduction from his bank account every month proved it. That could only mean she didn't care.

Everything from junk mail to clothes to dirty plates littered the floor. Cockroaches and ants swarmed old cans of fruit cocktail and soda left on the coffee table. The hall carpet was stained with only God knew what. Brady turned as Dana gave a muffled squeak and pointed to a decaying rat in the corner of the room.

Ollie walked over to the rodent as if it were nothing, reaching down to grab the book that it had died on. She shook the rat off, as if her actions were the most natural thing for a five-year-old to do. Karen, meanwhile, was making it a point to crunch on as many bugs as she could on her way to her bedroom.

"Girls!" Dana was the first to come back to herself. She plucked a pristine Neiman Marcus bag out of the corner and checked to make sure it wasn't infested. "Bring enough clothes for next week. And you can each bring your books and your favorite toys." All three scrambled around, picking through the debris and stomping on bugs as they passed.

Dana started to walk down the hallway, but Brady put a hand out to stop her. He could feel the goose bumps on her forearm. "Wait," he said quietly.

"What for?" Dana gave him a surprised look.

"Bev might be still here." He didn't want to think about it, but there could be another reason for the stench in the house.

Dana covered her mouth and her eyes went wide. "You don't think she's—"

Brady shrugged. "I hope not, but let me check."

Brady did a quick search of the house, slowly opening doors, becoming more and more horrified at each discovery. The toilet was clogged, filled to the point of overflowing. No house got this bad overnight. And that meant the girls had been living in filth for who knew how long. He stopped at the last door, which he figured had to be the master bedroom. If Bev was in the house, she'd be here. With a deep breath, he pushed open the door.

Brady had thought himself beyond shock, but the sight of the bedroom floored him. Bev's room was straight out of *House Beautiful* magazine. Her king-size bed was covered in an elegant bronze and silver designer duvet. The carpet was new and thick. In one corner a state-of-the-art laptop computer lay open on a teak desk, almost as if the user was planning to come back any moment. Tiffany-style lamps graced both the nightstand and the desk.

Barely able to hide his disgust, Brady opened her closet. He wasn't acting as an officer of the county. He was the uncle of three girls who'd been forced to live in squalor. The contents of the closet only made him angrier. Cedar-lined walls protected neat rows of linen and silk suits. The shoes were equally impeccable, lined up with the toes all pointing forward. He did a quick search of the dresser—beautiful sweaters and underwear in a variety of colors filled the generous drawers to the brim.

Looking into the large gilt-edge mirror above the dresser, Brady saw another door. It had to be her bathroom. With slow and careful movements, he crossed the room and opened the door. Relief that Bev wasn't there was quickly followed by another burst of fury. The sink was made of flawless marble, as was the Jacuzzi tub surround. Brady flushed the toilet. What the hell was she thinking? He stepped out of the room and could hear Dana talking with the children.

"Don't you have any clean clothes?" Dana was asking.

"These are the cleanest we have," Karen explained. He could hear the shame in her voice. "Momma says that if it looks clean, then she doesn't have to wash it. These *look* clean. See?"

"That's okay," Dana's voice was soothing, though Brady could hear the rage beneath her controlled tone. "Just get your very favorite clothes and all the underwear that you can find and we'll wash them when we get home."

Home.

Brady could almost see Dana make the decision. Even though she'd only known him for less than a day, she was prepared to make a home for his nieces.

"Put that down," Brady told Dana. "I need to show you something."

Dana wordlessly followed his instructions, putting down the bag and trailing behind him.

DANA WASN'T SURE what Brady wanted to show her. It wasn't as if that part of the house could be any worse than what she had already experienced. It horrified her that the girls seemed so accustomed to the condition of the house that it appeared "normal." No wonder their clothes smelled clean to them. Brady led her to the master bedroom. He pushed open the door and gestured for her to enter.

"My God."

Brady yanked open the drawers, grabbing a handful of silk underwear, then moving to the closet. "Cedar-lined." He enunciated the words carefully. He didn't have to tell her the closet alone had cost a fortune.

"Doesn't look as if Bev planned to go anywhere permanently," Dana observed, running her hand over the silk duvet. She clicked on a lamp and a beautiful amber glow filled the room. "I wonder what happened?"

With a sudden movement, Brady whirled and slammed his fist into the luxurious wallpaper. The sound reverberated throughout the room. Dana wasn't sure what to do. If she knew him better she could take him by the hand and tell him she felt the same way. But she didn't know him. Nevertheless, she felt herself crossing over to him, her hands, seemingly of their volition, reaching out to gently knead the bunched muscles of his shoulders. He tried to shake off her touch, but she persisted.

She'd never done this before. Never touched a stranger in such an intimate way, and she was disturbed by how much she liked feeling the warmth of his body on the palms of her hands. She supposed that after all they'd been through, he was no longer a stranger. He leaned his forehead against the wall, and Dana found herself mirroring the pose—her forehead on his back, her arms moving to encircle his waist. He smelled as if he'd just stepped out of the shower. They stood that way for only a few seconds, then Brady pushed himself off the wall.

Embarrassed, Dana stepped away from him. "There's got to be some kind of explanation. Was Bev always like this?" She didn't want to sound accusing, but she couldn't help wondering how Brady had let this situation occur.

Brady sank down on the edge of bed and shook his head, his face tight and drawn. Dana could see self-recrimination in his eyes.

"Didn't you know?" Now, she *was* accusing.

"I should have," he muttered. "I should have tried harder to see them."

"But why didn't you? Why *didn't* you see them?"

There was a long pause. Finally, he said in a low voice, "It's very complicated. When Carson went to prison, our whole family changed." He stopped and then looked up at her. "That's not true. Our family changed after Carson married Bev. My dad died when I was a kid and Mom raised us alone. For twenty years, it was just the three of us. Even when we moved out, we didn't move far. We had a lot of good times with my mother, dropping by to visit a couple of times a week, having dinner with her on Sundays, then just like that—" Brady snapped his fingers "—Carson met Bev. They got married a day later. At first, Bev seemed okay, but the longer they were together, the less Carson would see of my mother. His visits dropped off and soon there was only me and Mom for Sunday dinner. Even after

Karen was born, my mother rarely saw them. Bev made it so uncomfortable for her to visit them that she gave up after a while.''

Dana didn't say anything; her throat was too tight with emotion.

''Then my mom got sick. Really sick. Once she was diagnosed with lung cancer, she only lasted four months. Carson visited twice. She asked about him, Karen and Jean every day. Jean was only a baby and my mother never got to see her. The truth is I never forgave Carson for that, never forgave him for letting our mother die without bothering to say goodbye.''

His back straightened and he stared at Dana. ''You've got to believe me,'' he said roughly. ''I didn't like Bev, but I never thought she'd abuse her children. I never thought that she would do—this.''

He seemed to be pleading with her to understand.

Dana didn't know if she could. She still didn't understand what this had to do with Carson's children. Why hadn't he looked out for the girls after his brother's imprisonment? There had to be more to cause this long a rift. Brady wasn't telling her something. He wasn't telling her something big.

But she didn't have time to delve into this further. They needed to get the children out now.

"You know we can't let her have them back," Brady said, his voice pointed and urgent. "I won't let them go to CPS. I can't do that to Carson. It's bad enough that he's where he is. I'm not going to let those little girls get split up. I need your answer. Will you marry me?"

Dana felt his intensity—knew it was valid—but she couldn't stop remembering the last time she'd gotten involved. The last time she'd done something that defied common sense. If she hadn't loved Adam so much, he wouldn't be dead today. He would have never called her "Mommy." Instead of answering Brady, she headed for the door. "Come on. Let's find the girls and get out of here."

He caught her arm. "Dana, I need an answer. If you don't marry me, I'm going to have to find a family that's willing to take all three children so CPS doesn't have to be called. I don't know anyone. I know a lot of people, but no one who can handle *three*."

Dana met his eyes. "What makes you think I can?"

Brady drew her closer, and although her mind

resisted, her body complied. "Because of the way you are with them."

"I'm doing what anyone else in this situation would do." Her words sounded mechanical.

"Please, Dana."

She was going to do it. Against her better judgment, despite the fact she'd known the man less than twenty-four hours, she was going to marry him. Not because of him, but for Karen, Jean and Ollie. She pulled her arm out of his grasp. "We'll talk about it later."

She hurried out to the living room, intent on gathering up the girls and getting out of the house. She needed to process what she knew she would inevitably agree to.

There was no sign of the girls at all. She checked outside and then went back through the house.

"Karen?" she called as she checked the bedrooms. "Jean? Ollie?"

Brady joined her. "What's wrong?"

"I can't find the girls."

"They can't go far," Brady said.

"The kitchen?"

Brady started in that direction, but Dana ran past him. She pushed open the swinging door and stopped to find the girls huddled in the corner by the stove. Karen's arms were wrapped protectively around Ollie, and Jean, in a tight ball, rocked steadily on the other side of Ollie. All three were sobbing as if their hearts were breaking.

Dana immediately dropped to her knees. "What's wrong?"

"Is anyone hurt?" Brady asked as he stepped into the kitchen.

"Momma," Ollie sniffled.

"Momma?" The fine hairs on the back of Dana's neck stood up. "Are you remembering something about your mother?" Dana tried to pick up Ollie, but Karen wouldn't let go of her youngest sister.

Giving up, Dana rubbed one hand on Karen's back and motioned Brady over with the other. He knelt beside her, then pulled both girls into his arms.

Still on her knees, Dana turned to Jean.

Eyes squeezed shut, Jean keened like a wounded creature. When Dana laid a light hand on Jean's leg, Jean kicked out and scrambled away until she was under the table. Once there, she curled up in the fetal position and began to rock.

Dana went flat on her belly on the grimy floor

and inched toward the little girl. Finally, she was nose to nose with Jean and said, "Hey there, sweetie."

Jean whimpered and rocked harder.

"If you open just one eye, you'll see me. And I'll be smiling at you." Dana told her in a calm, low voice.

Jean shook her head, but the rocking slowed.

"One little-bitty eye," Dana persuaded. "I promise you'll just see me. And I'm smiling at you."

One blue eye opened. And then the little girl couldn't get into Dana's arms fast enough. "Shh, sweetie. You're safe with me. You're just fine. Karen's here, Ollie's here and Uncle Brady's here. We're all here."

"Momma's here, too," Ollie sniffed, her little finger pointing to a door that no doubt led to the garage.

CHAPTER FIVE

DANA EXCHANGED GLANCES with Brady. Then they both turned to stare at the door.

"Maybe you should take the girls out," Brady suggested.

Dana agreed. If Bev was behind that door, she preferred not to see her.

"Come on, sweeties. Let's go." She stood up awkwardly with Jean still clinging to her, then took Ollie's hand. "Karen, grab that bag and come with me."

Karen did what she was told, but the entire way across the kitchen, she looked over her shoulder at her uncle.

Dana left the house as quickly as she could, not wanting the girls to see how shaken she was. Once they got to the car, Dana opened all four doors. Ollie climbed into the back seat, and Dana leaned against the trunk, holding Jean. Karen joined Dana, never releasing her grip on their bag of belongings. Almost twenty minutes passed before Brady came outside, his mouth set in a grim, straight line.

"Is she…"

"Yes." His voice was low. "They're sending out the medical examiner."

"Medical examiner." Dana didn't want to know any more details. Before she could ask what they should do next, Brady grabbed the bag out of Karen's hands.

"What are you doing?" Dana asked.

"Something moved," he replied angrily, the muscle in his jaw jumping. He looked like he wanted to hurl the bag as far away as he could.

Dana took the bag from him and looked inside. All she saw was dirty underwear and grubby stuffed animals.

"I don't see anything," she said, gingerly sifting through the bag. "So it's not likely a rodent or anything. Maybe you saw a daddy longlegs. I'll just put the bag in the trunk."

"No." He pried Dana's fingers from the bag and proceeded to dump the contents onto the driveway. He ignored the horrified gasps from the little girls as he started to sort through the pile, looking for God only knew what.

Dana shifted Jean to her hip and said gently,

"Don't do that. There's nothing there. Anything big would have run away."

He disregarded her comment and continued to flick aside little shirts and pants. "We'd better do this or you'll be facing an infestation of your own."

"Stop it!"

The bark in Dana's voice finally got through to him. She couldn't believe he was so clueless that in front of the girls he would go through their things so callously. Such an inspection might be routine for him, but how could he not sense what it meant to his nieces?

Brady looked up, and she could still see the anger simmering in his eyes. She understood his anger and felt something similar herself, but this was not the way to vent it. With Jean still clinging to her like a koala bear, Dana bent down and put a firm hand on his arm to keep him from going through the clothes anymore.

Brady tried to jerk his arm away, but Dana hung on. For good measure she squeezed hard enough for him to wince.

She released her grip and trailed her hand up to his shoulder. She could feel the muscles bunched up as if he was ready to strike something, someone.

"Don't take it out on them." She gave him a pointed look, gesturing at his hands, which wrung a dingy pink shirt so hard his knuckles showed white.

DANA'S GRIP finally registered with Brady.

"What?" he asked, shaking the fog from his head. He looked down at his hands, surprised to find that he held a little shirt. He relaxed his grip, then tried to smooth out the wrinkles he'd made. He might not have liked Bev, but he'd never wished her ill. Finding her dead had been the last thing he'd expected. With no other sign of foul play, Brady had come to one painful conclusion. He'd called it in and then looked around, careful not to touch anything. Until the medical examiner declared the death a suicide, it was a crime scene. So now he was taking out his anger on a bag of clothes—all because he didn't have anything else to do.

"The girls are watching." Dana kept her tone low, but her meaning pierced his gut. "Don't embarrass them."

He turned his head. Sure enough, Karen, Jean and Ollie had their eyes glued to him. Tears ran down the faces of the younger girls, but Karen stepped forward, her chin thrust out.

"I *told* you the house wasn't clean," Karen accused Dana, her earlier suspicion toward him in her eyes. Brady felt his heart twist. He needed to be more careful with these fragile girls.

"Everything's fine," Dana replied. "Uncle Brady's just worried about whether it's safe for you to wear these clothes."

"He called us an in-infestation." Karen's bottom lip began to tremble, her suspicion turned into hurt.

Brady went right to Karen. She looked so small, so vulnerable. "I wasn't talking about you," he reassured her, putting a hand on her arm.

Karen clamped her lips tight, but she didn't shake off his hand. "I heard you call us an infestation."

He felt Dana's hand on his shoulder, a slight pressure signaling him to kneel down. She was right, he realized. He was towering over Karen. He crouched until he was eye to eye with the girl. "I wasn't talking about you. You aren't an infestation. You're little girls."

"You're showing our *underwear!*" Bright spots of red showed on her thin cheeks.

"Not anymore," Dana said, shoving the clothes back into the bag and then depositing it in the trunk. With a decisive push on the lid, she faced him and said, "We'll get them all nice and clean when we get home."

Before he could thank her for saving him yet again, Karen spoke. "Is Momma dead?"

After an awkward pause, Brady nodded. "I'm sorry, girls."

Ollie crawled out of the car, and Jean began to sob. Dana put Jean down so she could pull both girls close. Karen's face twisted with sadness, but she clearly wasn't going to give in to her grief yet.

"What's going to happen to us?" she asked.

"I don't know," Brady said honestly. "But I'm going to do my best to take care of you."

Karen nodded, but didn't look as if she believed him. Back straight, she turned away and got into the car. Heart breaking, Dana watched her go. After a moment she stood and announced, her voice firm, "We're going to go home. That's okay, right?"

Without waiting for an answer, she ushered Ollie and Jean into the back seat of the car. Happy to finally be useful, Brady strode to the passenger side of the car and closed those doors. He came back to the driver's side as Dana slid into the seat.

"Thanks," she said, searching through her purse looking for her car keys. "Is it okay for us to go? I don't think the children need to be here."

Brady nodded. "The police might want to talk to the girls, but that can be done at your place later."

Dana shook her purse, muttering under her breath.

"Are you okay?" Brady asked.

"I'm fine," she said, but her hand shook so much that when she pulled out her keys she dropped them.

"I'll get them," he offered as she fumbled between her legs.

"No, no," she insisted, her hand hitting his.

He gave her a brief squeeze before picking up the keys. "Here. I have them."

"Thanks." This time Dana got the keys in the ignition on the first try. She started the engine, then stomped on the gas, making the engine roar.

"Are you going to be able to drive?"

She took a deep breath and seemed to gain control. Giving him a weak smile, she said, "It's not far. Frankly, *I've* got to get away."

"If you want, I can run you all home and then come back here to finish up."

For a moment, Brady thought she was going to take him up on the offer, but then she put the car in reverse. "No, you've got work to do. When you're done, you'll come home, right?"

Home.

What a precious word. After his father died, his mother had done everything in her power to provide her children a loving home. She'd always gone over the top for the holidays and worked irregular shifts so that she could attend their ball games and after-school activities.

It was at home that Edie Moore had taught her sons self-sufficiency. Brady and Carson had learned to cook as soon as they were tall enough to flip pancakes. They'd done their own laundry and pitched in to keep the small house clean. His devotion to his mother had been strong. Even after he'd moved out, he still thought of his mother's house as home.

For the first time since his mother had died, Brady saw himself living in a home, Dana's home. It was an opportunity he didn't deserve, especially not with such a gentle woman who'd enveloped the children with her love, and if he wasn't careful, he'd be next.

He knew he'd taken too long to answer her. He could feel her eyes searching his face. God, she was pretty. Surprising himself, he leaned into the car and kissed her on the forehead. When his lips made contact with her smooth skin, he pulled back, uncertain about his own motives.

"Yes," he said, firmly shutting her door. "I will."

He jammed his hands into his pockets and watched Dana back out the driveway. Home. He'd see her again at home.

ONCE BACK at the little cottage, Dana gave the girls a small snack of cheese and crackers with apple juice, which Ollie and Jean munched on eagerly. Karen wasn't interested in the food. She just drank some juice and played with a cube of cheddar. To distract her, while Jean and Ollie ate, Dana asked Karen to help organize the guest room. Together they moved all the excess school supplies into the hall. Dana would find space for it all at the school. Then they cleared papers off the desk so the girls would have someplace to do homework. Finally they emptied out all the dresser drawers, dumping the contents into garbage bags. Dana was just moving the garbage bags to the garage when the doorbell rang.

Two officers waited on her front step. As she opened the door, she wished Brady was there. His strength would make what was coming much more bearable. Steeling herself for the ordeal, Dana showed the officers into the living room and then went to get the children. Once the interview started, Dana began to relax slightly. The officers were professional, posing gentle questions about their life with Bev Moore. They asked Karen the most questions and she answered every one calmly. The interview was just coming to a close when Brady arrived. He spoke to his colleagues for a moment, then showed them to the door.

"I'm so glad you're here," Dana said after the officers left.

"I'm not here for long. I've got to go back, but I wanted to make sure you were doing okay. You look as if you've survived."

"Uncle Brady, I want to see Momma," Karen said before she could speak.

Dana hedged. "I'm not sure—"

"We need to see her. We need to say goodbye."

"It's okay, Dana." Brady was standing right behind her, his hand on her shoulder, kneading gently. His touch felt good—felt *right*—and she wondered why. "If the girls want to see their mother, they should. But not right now."

"When?" Karen asked.

"I don't know. Probably in a couple of days. We're trying to figure out what happened to her, so you can't see her until we do."

Karen nodded in obvious understanding. In a

manner much too mature for an eleven-year-old, she took her sisters' hands and said, "We'd like to be alone now."

Dana and Brady watched the girls walk down the hall to the guest room.

Once the door closed she turned to Brady. "Are you sure their seeing Bev is a good idea?" She'd had the opportunity to see Adam, but she'd declined. She couldn't have handled seeing her sweet, laughing boy that way.

Brady searched her face before replying in a low voice, "If the girls want to go, we shouldn't stop them. Everyone should have a chance to say goodbye."

Dana swallowed and crossed her arms over her chest to hold back the feelings that were beginning to overwhelm her. She fought to retain control. For years she'd kept her memories of Adam at bay, but as she'd feared, caring for these children had torn down all her defenses.

"Dana. Are you okay?" Suddenly Brady was next to her, guiding her over to the couch, easing her down.

"No," she gasped. "I'm not okay."

She put her head on her knees. "I can't do this, I can't do this for you," she choked out.

"Do what, Dana?"

She felt his hand on the top of her head, but she couldn't speak. If she opened her mouth, she'd lose the fight and then everything would come bubbling up.

"What is it, Dana? What is it you can't do?"

"I'm not going to care." The words flew out of her, and all her fears came to life. "I cared for Adam, and what did it get me? Grief. Pain. I won't do it. I *can't.*"

She could hear a phone ringing. Was it hers? She should answer it. Why wasn't Brady answering it? But Dana only heard a phantom from long ago. She'd been in the bath, reading a book.

"Hello?"

"Miss Ritchie? Dana Ritchie?"

"Mrs. Johnson? What's wrong? Is Adam okay?"

"He will be now."

The gleeful tone in the woman's voice scared Dana. "What are you talking about? Let me talk with Adam."

"No. He's not yours. You can't have him."

"I know he's not mine. He's his own person."

"All he does is talk about you. He talks about you as if you're his mother. You're not his mother. I am!"

Dana had tried to stay calm. "Please, Mrs. Johnson, let me talk to Adam."

"You can't talk to him. He's a bad boy. A bad, bad boy."

"No. He isn't bad. Adam's a good boy."

"He won't stop crying. He just cries and cries and cries. And you know what happens to bad boys who don't stop crying."

And then with the bathwater cooling around her, Dana had heard the sounds of a disturbed woman ending her child's life.

BRADY DIDN'T KNOW what was happening, but he realized that Dana was suffering. He held her close, his heart beating rapidly. He didn't know what else to do. Then he remembered how she'd comforted Jean.

He pressed her head to his chest and murmured, "You're safe. You're okay."

Dana hung on to him as if her life was at stake. He closed his eyes and rested his cheek on the top of her head just repeating that mantra, "You're safe. You're okay."

Some time later, her crying subsided. "I'm sorry," Brady said, voice soft, knowing his words were inadequate.

Dana shook her head and pulled herself out of his embrace, looking very fragile and frightened.

"Don't be sorry," she said, her voice tentative. "This isn't about you. I'm the one who should be sorry. I didn't mean to do that."

"Do you want to talk about it?" Brady asked.

Dana shook her head. "No. It's something that's better left in the past."

"*It* doesn't appear to realize that," he observed.

She shrugged. "It'll be fine. If it wasn't for—for—all of this…"

"It's not something that happens every day," he said with a nod. "Your reaction is perfectly normal."

She gave a small laugh. "Hardly normal. Nothing's been normal since I met you."

Brady cleared his throat. "It's not always going to be like this. In fact, it should be easier from now on."

"Easier?" She didn't look as if she believed him.

'But given the circumstances, I would understand if you don't want to get married.''

She didn't speak, didn't move. The moment stretched as she just stared at him, giving no clue as to what she was thinking. "Say something," he prompted.

"Like what?" Her voice was tense.

"Like…I don't know. Just don't be silent."

She sucked in a noisy breath. "Doesn't guardianship revert to you as their next of kin? Then you won't need me. After all, you only wanted to get married so Bev couldn't take the children when she got back. Obviously, that's not an issue."

Brady tried to quell the feelings of disappointment that began to creep through him. She was looking for a way out, and he didn't blame her one bit. Three abandoned children, a dead mother, a house that he wouldn't wish on his worst enemy. If he was her, he'd run as fast as he could.

He just hoped she was made of sterner stuff than he was. "I wish it was that easy. I would eventually get them, but I still don't have room for them. And I'm a bachelor. The state is going to be cautious about leaving three girls with me."

"You're a deputy sheriff!" Dana said indignantly. "You're the last person that would hurt those girls."

He continued as if she'd never spoken, "There'd be no problem if I had a wife, a real home. But I don't.'' He looked at her meaning-fully.

The pause lasted a long time.

"You have the home," he ventured.

"I do."

Brady's heart pounded in his ears. "There's no good reason in the world why you should do this—"

"What about your brother?" Her question took him by surprise.

"What about him?"

"You'll have to tell him what's happened."

"I'll get a message to him."

"You're going to let a stranger tell him his wife is dead? And that before she died she neglected his children?" Dana was looking at him as if he'd lost his mind. "No. Before we do anything, you need to explain all this to him. He has every right to know."

"If you still agree, we'll get married tomorrow and then I'll see him on Monday." Brady wanted to put that off for as long as possible.

"Do we need to get married tomorrow?"

He shook his head. "But the sooner the better."

"Then why couldn't we wait until Friday?"

"Friday." Brady swallowed. Why was it that

conversations with Dana never seemed to go in the direction that he wanted?

"Aren't Sundays traditional visiting days for prisons?"

"I can get in anytime," he admitted.

"Then I suggest that tomorrow you visit your brother, discuss the situation, and then—"

He wanted to talk about something else. "If we don't get married until Friday, I wouldn't expect you to keep the girls alone for the next week."

"And you would do what? Hire a nanny?" Her lips twisted into a small smile.

What would he do? The words were out of his mouth before he could stop them. "I could stay with you. The girls are going through a very rough time. It would be better if they were with us, rather than a foster family. I have plenty of vacation time. I'll take some until we get organized. Then, when I go back to work, we can figure out some sort of schedule."

Her face didn't register the surprise he'd anticipated it would. In fact, she seemed to be running the scenario through her mind.

"Where would you sleep?" Her voice was soft, and Brady suddenly realized how close they were sitting to each other.

"The couch, of course." He nonchalantly patted the couch.

She frowned. "And after we're married?"

Brady chuckled. He couldn't help it. The thought of sharing her bed was something he hadn't considered until this very moment.

"Well, that's not very flattering," she said, but her lips twitched and then lifted into a glorious smile.

"It wasn't that." Brady tried to make up for laughing, though she wasn't really offended. "I just—"

A few minutes ago, before she smiled, he'd been thinking about this arrangement in a purely clinical way. She wasn't his type. Usually, he favored easygoing and uncomplicated women. While she might fit the first part, she definitely didn't fit the second. Yet, that smile and those deep brown eyes of hers had somehow managed to grab his heart.

He changed the subject. "I'll do the shopping and the cooking and watch the girls after school until we all get settled in."

She frowned. "I don't even know you."

He laughed. "Don't you think we've been through enough to make up for a couple of years of getting to know each other?" Then he continued, all lightness gone, "I can't let them go to Social Services. Even if they let me take the girls, and I found another place for all of us to stay, they would be starting a different school in the middle of the year. They like you. Please help us."

Brady watched Dana battle something inside her. If she thought she'd masked her inner turmoil, she was mistaken. But a moment later she nodded and said, "Okay."

"Okay? What does okay mean?"

"Okay, you can stay here. Okay, I'll marry you on Friday. You'll fix it with your friends so we're not breaking any laws?"

"Yes."

"Then it's done." She was nodding again, almost as if she was convincing herself that she was doing the right thing. For a moment they just looked at each other, then she leaned forward to kiss him lightly on the lips.

Before he could respond, she pulled away and stood up, saying briskly, "Don't you need to get back?"

Brady exhaled in relief. "Yes. And, Dana, thank you."

But she was already halfway down the hall.

CHAPTER SIX

DANA SCROUNGED AROUND in the freezer for something that resembled a dinner. Karen again picked at her food, but Dana didn't press her. After the dishes were done, she sent the three girls into the tub. Considering the day they'd had, she was surprised but very pleased to hear playful splashing after a while.

She felt a curious sense of anticipation, almost as if she was looking forward to this new path her life was taking. But she knew she was being ridiculous. Didn't she ever learn? She had to use this situation, this *marriage,* as a test, an exercise to prove she could keep duty and emotion separate. These weren't her girls. And their uncle was just a nice man she was helping out. That's all. It wasn't as if she liked *him* or anything. Her face grew warm at the memory of how it had felt to put her arms around his waist and rest her head on his back.

"Silly." She shook her head. She was too old

to start doing this kind of speculating, way too old. The trouble was she *did* like him. She liked the fact he was willing to marry a stranger to help the girls. And that he was careful and precise and listened to her. She liked the way he looked at her as if she was actually pretty. And there was no denying she liked the fact he'd kissed her. Granted, it had been a brotherly, affectionate kind of kiss, not one of grand passion, but it had still managed to send shivers down her spine.

There was a sharp rap on the front door and by the time she got there, Brady was already poking his head in.

"Don't you ever lock this door?" he asked as he walked in, holding a paper bag.

"Is that all you have?" Dana asked.

He shrugged. "This is all I need for tonight." He reached in and pulled out a brand-new toothbrush, razors and deodorant.

"I have extras. You didn't have to buy them."

"Don't want to impose. I'll get the rest of my stuff tomorrow."

Dana didn't know where he'd put the "rest" or even how much that was. She looked around the living room for a nook where he'd be able to stash his belongings. "Would that corner be okay for your things?" she offered.

He nodded.

Karen came out of the bathroom wearing one of Dana's old T-shirts that hung past her knees. Jean and Ollie followed her out, having to pick up their T-shirts to avoid tripping over the hems.

"What's *he* doing here?"

Dana was oddly embarrassed by Karen's question. "He's going to help take care of you," she explained.

"He can't stay." Karen was appalled.

"Well, he is." And Dana was very glad that he was.

"But—"

"But?" Dana asked.

"He's a *boy,*" Karen said in a scandalized whisper.

"I know that."

"We're girls. We don't want boys living with us."

"He's different."

"He can't see us, you know—" She jerked her head toward the bathroom.

"I'll be in charge of all the baths."

Karen nodded, but didn't look convinced. With one last glance at Brady, she motioned to her sisters and hustled into the bedroom.

"It's good to know that I have the ability to chase away small girls," he said dryly.

"They'll get used to you. They're probably not used to men," Dana said. "Do you need anything?"

He shook his head. "I tell you. I travel light."

They stared at each other for a long moment. Then they both laughed. "Now what?" she asked.

"Does the television work?" He pointed to it.

Dana stared at the set in her living room. "Yes, it does. I don't watch too much, but feel free. I keep the remote here."

"That's all I need to know."

"We're going to have to tell the girls."

"About?" He sat down on the couch and rested his head against it, holding the remote, but not turning on the television.

"About us getting married."

He nodded. "Tomorrow is soon enough, don't you think?"

Dana perched on the arm of the couch. "Yes. If you're hungry, there's stuff in the freezer or canned goods under the counter. The fridge is pretty bare, though."

He nodded again, but Dana realized that he was studying her with great intent.

"What? Do I have something on my face?"

"No."

"What then?"

"Nothing. I was just wondering what kind of woman marries a man she doesn't love."

"A crazy one," Dana said. "We probably shouldn't talk about it, because I'll get a case of the jitters and back out."

He reached out and caught her hand, then tugged to indicate that he wanted her to sit next to him. Dana complied, finding that her heart had lodged in her throat. They gazed at each other for a long time. With his right hand, Brady traced her hairline. "Why is it we haven't met before this?" he mused, his voice husky.

"I work too hard to meet anyone," she said. Her nerves were on fire wherever he touched her. After a moment, he put his hand behind her neck and slowly urged her closer until his lips were on hers.

Dana felt herself sink into him, sure that if she pulled away, he would let her go. But she was also sure that if she deepened the kiss, he wouldn't mind. She chose to deepen the kiss and wasn't disappointed. Even as he pressed her back against the couch Dana felt as if this was what she was made for.

All too soon he was pulling away, a smile on his face. Dana moaned in protest. "Why are you stopping?" She needed the kiss, wanted the contact.

"It's been a long day. I'm afraid that if I go farther, I wouldn't want to stop."

She tilted her head. "I don't think I would object."

"If we're really going to be married on Friday, we can wait. Besides, if we do this, I want you to be very sure. After this is over, I don't want you to be hurt."

"After this is over?" She swallowed hard.

He nodded. "You know, when I have everything together and can care for the girls by myself."

Dana looked away, feeling a sharp stab in her stomach.

"Dana—" his voice was filled with concern "—I don't want you to think this marriage is going to be something that will tie you down forever. I know you're doing me a huge favor. I'll try to get a new place as soon as possible. I'm sure we'll be able to get the marriage annulled before Christmas."

"And what if I don't want to have it annulled?" she asked, her tone light. "What if I fall in love with you and the girls and we find that we make this the perfect family?''

Brady was silent. Then he shook his head. ''The odds of that happening are very slim.''

''Why?''

''We don't even know each other. You may find that in two weeks you can't stand the sight of me.''

His answer wasn't satisfying. How could he kiss her like that and not know her?

''Well, we can figure all this out later.''

''Dana, I'm sorry if I've disappointed you.''

Dana got up. ''You haven't disappointed me. Not at all.'' But she was lying.

IT DIDN'T TAKE LONG for Dana to prepare for bed. She checked on the girls and was glad to see they were asleep. She knew they were very, very tired. Unfortunately, sleep was far more elusive for her. She lay awake, eyes wide open, hearing every move Brady made. First he went into the kitchen for some water, then he went down the hall and out the door. She counted to one hundred and forty-five before he came back.

It was odd knowing there were four other people in her house. She'd slept alone here every night since she'd moved in. Maybe that was why she was having so much trouble sleeping. She concentrated on her breathing, but within seconds her mind was wandering to the kiss they'd shared on the couch. He could talk about her hating him after two weeks, but she knew that wasn't going happen. Was she insane to marry him? It would help the girls and help Brady. But what about her? Somehow she knew when this was all over, there'd be no one around to help her.

THE NEXT MORNING, Dana awoke to her alarm. She peered at the clock. It said five-twenty. She groaned and rolled over. It was Sunday. She didn't have to get up. But try as she did to go back to sleep, she couldn't. Her mind had become fixated on the kiss. What had possessed her? To *touch* Brady Moore was bolder than anything she'd ever thought herself capable of. And then to *kiss* him…

After a half hour, she finally got out of bed and pulled on her robe.

Brady slept on his back with one arm slung over his face and one foot planted on the floor— as if even in sleep he would be able to leap up at a moment's notice. As quietly as she could, Dana put water on for tea. When she turned around again, Brady was sitting up, his face in his hands.

"Good morning!" Dana greeted, her voice sounding a little too loud.

He winced.

"Sorry," she said much more quietly.

He waved off her apology. "I'm not a morning person. It takes me about an hour to get started." His voice rumbled out of his chest, all gravelly again. "It's probably why I take the night shift. What time is it?" He squinted at his watch.

"About six."

"In the morning?" He yawned again, and then fell back on the couch. "Are you always this cheerful in the morning?"

Dana grinned. "Yep. Would coffee help?"

"Coffee will save my life."

"Coming up."

"Thanks," he grunted, standing up and reaching for his shirt.

Dana ducked her head. Even unshaven, Brady Moore had a powerful presence. "Did you sleep okay?" Her question was muffled.

"Yes, the couch is plenty comfortable."

"Maybe for a night or two, but for a longer period of time…" She ventured a look up, relieved to see he'd put on his shirt. Not that a shirt made him any less attractive.

"Are you offering me different sleeping accommodations?'' he inquired, raising a dark eyebrow.

"No!" popped out so fast that Dana covered her mouth in shock. "I was just worried about your back."

"My back and I are fine. But what about you? You're still okay with this, right? Tomorrow, I'm going to get a lawyer and make the final arrangements for the ceremony." As he spoke, Brady came into the kitchen. Not seeming to notice that she wasn't responding, he leaned over her to get a cup from the cabinet. It took all of Dana's willpower to prevent herself from burying her face in his soft cotton shirt.

"You'll be ready to get married Friday, right?"

"I hadn't really thought about it." It was a complete lie, of course. She'd fallen asleep thinking about it and woken up thinking about it.

"Good." He looked at the clock. "I'll start something for breakfast, you wake up the girls."

He gave her a gentle nudge in the direction of the hall.

If she didn't know better, she would have sworn he was considering giving her a peck on the lips. She touched them, feeling as if he had.

As Dana went to wake up the girls, she could hear Brady clattering around in the kitchen. She didn't know if she had anything that even resembled breakfast food, let alone enough to feed five people. The girls rose with energy Dana envied. While she was still trying to figure out what day it was, they hopped around the living room in her T-shirts, before settling down to watch a half hour of cartoons.

The scene that greeted Dana after her shower was so normal-looking she actually had to remind herself that nothing about this situation was normal. *And* that it was temporary. Temporary was the key word. They would get married and when Brady found a place to accommodate all three girls, they would leave. And where would she be? Teaching, grading papers and filling out forms.

At the table, Brady seemed surprisingly relaxed, given that in the time it had taken her to wake the girls, take a shower and dress, he'd made waffles, sausage and scrambled eggs. Orange juice was in five mismatched cups.

"Wow," she said. "I didn't even know I had a waffle iron."

"It was way in the back of the cupboard," he said. "I was scoping through your stuff and saw it."

"Sausage?"

"Freezer."

Dim memories of a parent giving her bulk sausage from their farm last Christmas surfaced. "You're magic."

He looked pleased with himself and called the girls to the table. Compared to the meals that she'd fixed, this was a culinary masterpiece. Brady not only served, but focused special attention on each girl. Jean and Ollie beamed, becoming all smiles and giggles. Karen, however, was subdued as she poured a modest amount of syrup on her waffle and then used her fork to distribute the syrup into each little crater.

"It's okay to be sad, Karen," Dana said, covering the girl's hand with her own.

"I just can't believe she did that. Why would she hurt herself?"

Dana and Brady exchanged glances.

Brady finally broached the difficult subject. "We don't know for sure that she did, do we?"

Karen stared at her plate for a moment, then looked up and shook her head. Dana could tell Karen wanted to say something else, but didn't know where to start. Brady must have noticed, too, because suddenly he asked, "Do you know why she would do something like that?"

Tears started to roll down Karen's face, making Jean and Ollie stop eating. Murmuring soothing words, Dana pulled Karen into her arms and let her cry.

"M-mon-ey," Karen finally got out when she could talk again.

"Money?" Dana asked, her voice calm. "What does money have to do with it?"

"She said we were expensive and that's why she was in so much debt."

Brady remained silent, obviously aware that Karen responded better to Dana's gentle probing. "Your mom was in debt?"

Karen nodded, miserable. "A while ago I heard her talking on the phone. But then she stopped answering it. It would ring and ring and ring all the time. Finally she made me pick it up and tell the people that she wasn't home."

"She liked cards," Ollie told them.

Karen shot a furious look at Ollie. "That's a secret."

"How can cards be a secret?" Dana asked, knowing that Brady would want her to follow this thread.

With big, sad eyes, Ollie said, "I forgot. We weren't supposed to tell."

Karen seemed to forgive her sister, because she sighed and began to explain. "You know. They were card games that she played on the Internet. She's not going to get into more trouble, is she?''

''I don't think so. I think that your mom's troubles are finally over,'' Dana said.

''What's going to happen to us? Are we going to have to go to an orphanage?'' Karen asked.

''Not if we can help it,'' Brady said at last.

''Are you going to take us?'' Karen looked hopeful.

''In a way. Actually we both are.''

''Both of you?'' Ollie stood up in her chair and leaned forward.

''Sit down, Ollie,'' Dana said automatically, putting a hand out to steady her as she sat back down. ''Yes, both of us. We're going to get married on Friday, so you can stay here until your Uncle Brady finds a place for all of you to live.''

Karen's eyes went wide and then filled with tears. In an attempt to soothe her, Dana said, ''I know this is all happening very fast. But we're not going to try to be your mom and dad.''

Karen shook her head. ''I used to pray that you'd be our mother. You were always so nice to us. I loved my momma but she didn't love us back.''

Dana didn't know what to say. This sweet girl was giving so much of herself, but Dana couldn't do the same. Brady kept telling her this was only temporary. If she gave her love to these children and then had to watch them walk away, she might never recover. But how was she ever going to resist these three girls.

BRADY SAT in the gray room with gray walls and gray floors. Slivers of sunlight passed through a row of narrow windows large enough to let in light but not big enough for even a child to squeeze through. Brady scrubbed a hand across his face. He'd hardly slept in the past forty-eight hours and he had what felt like the world's biggest hangover, without even the memory of a good party to make him feel better. He tried to shift back into a more comfortable position only to be reminded that the utilitarian chair was bolted to the floor, as was the steel table. This might be a minimum-security prison, but it *was* still a prison.

Telling his brother what had happened to Bev and the children was simply one more unpleasant task in a long series of unpleasant tasks. The quicker he did it the better. He didn't want to chat about the weather, didn't want to ask how his brother was doing. Shame—in the form of a chiding voice that sounded an awful lot like the woman who had opened her household to his nieces and himself—nudged his conscience for not making the trip earlier. Brady closed his eyes and pretended he wasn't affected by the fact that this drive had taken him two hours and five years to make.

A buzzing sound told him the door was being unlocked. Brady stood and slowly turned, his heart hammering right behind his eyes. Carson looked so different, Brady almost didn't recognize him. He'd always been quiet and serious, but now he seemed so guarded that Brady got the feeling his brother was always ready to strike the first blow.

"What do you want?" Carson asked, sitting in the chair on the other side of the table.

Good. Just the way Brady wanted it, short and to the point. But somehow he didn't know where to start.

"Come on," Carson continued. "I'm sure you're not here for the scenery."

"It's about the girls." Suddenly Brady didn't want to say what he needed to.

For the briefest of moments, Brady saw pain flash through his brother's eyes before he controlled it. "They're okay?" he asked.

"Yes. Now."

"What do you mean by that?"

"Bev's dead." He was blunt to the point of cruel, but there was no other way.

"Dead?" Carson gave Brady such a dark look that he began to feel as if this was somehow his fault.

"Suicide, they think."

Carson digested the information for a moment, then spoke a single word. "When?"

"Friday night, maybe yesterday morning."

Carson's face turned ash gray. "Where're the girls?"

"They're staying with their schoolteacher, Dana Ritchie. Bev left them with her on Friday afternoon. Dana called the sheriff's office and they got in touch with me. We found Bev the next day when we went to get some of the girls' clothes."

"Did she leave a note? Have any of her friends said why she would want to commit suicide?"

Brady shook his head. "We're still interviewing people."

"You're sure it's suicide."

Brady shrugged. "As far as we can tell. There were no signs of a struggle. The M.E.'s report will be more conclusive."

"The poor girls. They must be devastated."

Brady cleared his throat. "There's more."

"More?" Carson looked as if he didn't want to know about it.

"Uh, there were signs of neglect."

The shame he'd tried to ignore earlier burned through Brady as he watched the agony on his brother's face. Regardless of Carson's crimes, he wasn't a bad father. He loved his girls so much that he'd broken the law to keep their mother happy. Brady swallowed back the sympathy. Carson should have realized that no amount of money would make Bev happy.

"Neglect or abuse?" Carson asked after a moment.

"Physical abuse? She never hit them. Emotional abuse? Certainly. Neglect? Definitely. All too often the girls were left to fend for themselves. Karen's reluctant to say much, but what she has said tells us Bev could be gone for days at a time. Karen has taken care of her sisters as well as she could, but they lived in terrible circumstances."

Carson's mouth was tight when he said, "Tell me everything."

Brady did. "Their house was unbelievable. Bev's room was immaculate, while the kids lived in squalor. The toilet didn't work, and from the looks of it, hadn't been working for days. I know she had money, but she didn't spend any of it on the kids.''

''What's going to happen to the girls?''

''They're staying with their teacher until the end of the week. We're going to get married Friday and apply for temporary custody.''

Carson actually snorted.

''What?'' Brady couldn't keep the defensiveness out of his voice. ''It's the only way I could convince her to keep the children. I'm in a studio apartment and the kids would have to go to foster care until I could find a better place. One family member in the system is enough.''

''Have you known her long?''

''It doesn't matter how long I've known her.''

Carson stared at him. ''What does that mean?''

''Let's just say that we've become close, very quickly.''

''How many months?'' Carson persisted. ''These are my children, I have a right to know who's going to be taking care of them.''

Brady shook his head. ''I wouldn't say months. More like hours.''

''*Hours?* And you're going to marry her? I would have thought you'd learn from my mistakes. Look what a hasty marriage did to me.''

"It's not the same thing," Brady denied. "Dana's nothing like Beverly, nothing at all. It's true I don't love her, but she knows what she's getting into. She wants to help the kids. When I get settled, we'll annul the marriage."

"This is a bad idea."

"Would you rather see the kids in a foster home, split up? I can't do that to them." Brady stood up. "I didn't come to get your blessing. I just came to tell you about Bev and to let you know that the girls are going to be okay."

"Staying with strangers?"

"They'd be staying with strangers anyway. Hell, if you got out, you'd be a stranger to them." Brady immediately wanted to take back the words. "Sorry. I didn't have to say that."

Carson shrugged. "You're right. Bev promised to bring the kids by, but she rarely did."

The brothers stared at each other.

Finally Brady sat down again. "I know it seems weird, but I needed to have some way of not just protecting these girls, but to provide for them as well."

Carson was silent, then seemed to decide something. "Brady, I'm not guilty." It was a bald statement from a man who no longer had time for tact or finesse.

Brady sighed. This was exactly the conversation he didn't want to get into. "Carson, I don't want to hear it. Right now, you've done five of fifteen, I'm sure your lawyer has told you that you can be out in a couple of years."

"Then what?" Carson asked. His voice was urgent. "Are you going to give me back my girls? Or by then will you have full custody?"

Brady didn't want to think that far ahead. He just wanted the girls to have a clean, safe place to live.

"That will have to be figured out later. Karen, Jean and Ollie need a real family, not—"

"Their father? A felon."

It took Brady a long time to answer, but he looked directly into his brother's eyes and said, "Yes."

"No." Carson's voice was fierce. "These girls need me. They need their father. I agree that you and this woman should have temporary custody. But remember, they're my girls. I did not do anything wrong. I did not launder money. I did not embezzle from my clients. I did not fix my books. But somehow, I still went straight to jail. Don't you think that's kind of funny, given that my brother is a cop?"

Brady felt the blood rush to his head. He leaned

over the table, his voice low. "My being a cop doesn't have anything to do with the fact that your computer contained all the evidence they needed to convict you."

"This doesn't have anything to do with that," Carson said flatly.

"What do you mean?"

"This has to do with Mom."

"This has nothing to do with Mom."

"You've never forgiven me for not seeing her at the end."

If Brady was totally honest with himself, he'd admit that Carson's last words were true. But that didn't change what Carson had done. Getting up, he strode over to the door and rapped on it. The guard's head appeared in the window. Brady indicated that he wanted to leave.

"Don't you think that I haven't regretted that whole period of my life?" Carson asked. "Brady, I didn't do it. And if you wanted to, you could help me."

Brady pretended he didn't hear Carson's plea and walked out. He'd done his job. It was all he'd come for.

CHAPTER SEVEN

WHILE BRADY VISITED HIS brother, Dana washed
the girls' clothes. Even though it seemed as if
she'd hardly slept, she was filled with an energy
that was almost manic. The younger girls had
tried to help her, but their attention spans were
short. Mostly they bounced from room to room,
Ollie chattering nonstop, Jean following behind.

Karen had gone right back to bed after breakfast and hadn't come out since. It was late afternoon when Dana went in to check on her again,
only to find her wide awake, staring at the ceiling.
Without a word, Dana sat on the bed and ran a
gentle hand down Karen's cheek. Karen didn't
even acknowledge her presence. Dana just sat
there for a long time, brushing back the girl's fine
hair.

"Miss Ritchie?" Karen finally spoke.

"Yes?"

"Was my mom a bad person?" Her voice was

worried. "Does that mean she won't get to go to heaven?"

Dana wasn't sure how to answer that. Part of her did think Bev was a horrible person—how else could her treatment of the children be explained? "I think your mother was in a lot of pain and heaven is a place where pain is healed."

"Oh." Karen rolled over to her side, cradling her head with an arm. "Miss Ritchie?"

"Yes."

"Is it okay to miss her?"

Dana nodded, considering the earnest face. "I would worry about you if you didn't miss her."

Karen was quiet and then said, still staring straight ahead, "I didn't like her very much, but I miss her."

"And you're going to miss her for a long time. That's okay, you know. It's also okay to be mad at her and not to like her too much."

"She would always say she hated her life, that it was my dad's fault first, then ours. It was because we were so bad."

Dana quelled the burst of anger she felt. "That was her pain talking. She loved you very much. What happened to her has nothing to do with you. You and your sisters are very good people."

Karen sucked in a deep breath and tears started

to form in her eyes as she looked up at Dana. "Will we stay with Uncle Brady forever? Or will he leave us one day, too?"

"He really wants you to stay with him. He's definitely going to try to see that you live happily ever after."

"Is there really a happily-ever-after?" Karen's voice was wistful. "It doesn't feel like it. I don't think I'll be happy ever again."

Dana brushed the girl's hair back. "I know, sweetie. It's going to hurt for a long time. But it will get better. Time helps."

"Uncle Brady! Uncle Brady!" Squeals in the living room alerted them to Brady's arrival.

Dana looked down at the girl. "Do you want to get up? Just for a little bit?"

Karen shook her head. "I'd just rather stay here."

"I understand. But feel free to come out when you want to."

Dana left the room, gently shutting the door behind her. She had to quell a small sense of anticipation as she walked down the hall. Brady gave her a brief smile when she entered the living room. He had Ollie on his shoulders and the little girl was screaming with delight.

"How'd it go?" Dana asked.

He shrugged. "He knows. That's all that I went there for."

"Oh." Dana wanted more details, but remembered that she didn't really know him well enough to ask for them. And his evasiveness told her he wouldn't be forthcoming unless she did press him.

"I stopped by my apartment. Packed enough for the next few weeks." He lifted Ollie up and over his head and put her safely to the ground. Then he held his hands out to Jean who shyly stepped into them. And when he lifted her up, her small giggle was as filled with joy as Ollie's squeal had been.

"Do you want me to get your bags?" Dana offered.

"No. I've got them." He started in the direction of the door with Jean perched on his shoulders grabbing handfuls of his hair and Ollie skipping next to him. Dana watched from the front door as he put Jean down and pulled two duffel bags from the bed of his truck. Jean and Ollie, in a joint effort, grabbed one and proceeded to drag it toward the house. Dana smiled as the bag bumped against every uneven part of the pavement.

"I hope you don't have anything fragile in there," she commented as he walked in.

He looked over his shoulder, and Dana saw his lips tilt up in a smile. "Not anymore. The corner still okay for my stuff?"

Dana nodded. While he'd been gone, Dana had emptied out a spare dresser that had held linen and moved it to the corner for Brady's use. As Jean and Ollie finally managed to get themselves and the bag into the house, their laughter filling every corner, Dana realized how empty the house had been before. Or maybe she had been empty. Having the girls around didn't hurt the way she thought it would. But, she reminded herself, it wasn't the loving that hurt, it was the letting go.

AFTER THE GIRLS had gone to bed, Dana finally remembered she had school in the morning. She'd done nothing all weekend. She hadn't graded any of her students' work, she hadn't planned any of the assignments. She hadn't even stepped foot in the school.

Brady sat in front of the television, channel surfing. "Don't let me bother you," he said. "Just do what you would normally do."

Dana laughed. "You mean lesson plans and grading?"

"Yes, that." He lowered the volume on the television, presumably so it wouldn't disturb her.

Dana sat down and pulled out her assignment book. Funny, she couldn't even remember where they'd finished on Friday. Had that much time passed? A half hour later Dana put her papers down after realizing she'd been reading the same thing over and over again. She surreptitiously positioned herself to look at Brady. He was slouched, his neck resting on the back of the sofa, his stocking feet propped on the old coffee table. He looked asleep.

But then he glanced over his shoulder. Dana ducked her head. A minute passed and she ventured to look up again. He was staring at her.

"You okay?" she asked.

"Yes."

"Can I help you?" She sat up straighter and then stretched before walking over to the couch. After all, he was going to be her husband. She should feel comfortable enough to sit in the same room with him. "Anything interesting on?"

He shrugged. "Not really."

"Was it hard to see Carson?" Dana didn't know what had made her ask. She knew he didn't want to talk about it. For a minute, she didn't think he was going to answer her.

Finally, he said, "It's the first time I've seen Carson since he went in."

"Your decision or his?"

"A little of both. More mine than his." Brady looked at her. "He told me that he didn't do it."

"What do you think?"

Brady sighed and shook his head. "It was so long ago, I'm not sure what I think. I didn't want to believe it at first. I thought it was a big mistake. A good friend of mine was on the task force that was investigating a company that was one of Carson's main clients. We knew the company was shady, but we didn't know how. After they got the search warrant, they carried out all the computers. They took those computers apart."

He gave a small laugh. "One thing I learned about computers is that they save everything, even stuff you delete. You just need to know how to retrieve the information. Most of them were clean, but there was one that held proof of doctored accounting."

"Implicating Carson?"

Brady nodded. "He always said he didn't do it. But computers don't lie. He's a criminal. He deserves what he gets."

"But he's your brother." Dana couldn't help it. "Didn't you listen to his side of the story?"

"He's an adult. He didn't need my help."

"Are you so sure about that?"

He stared off into the middle distance. Finally, he met her eyes and Dana was struck by the pain she saw. "Yes. I am sure about that."

"Are you sure he did it?"

"He took a plea. Even his lawyer didn't think he had a very good case. So he went to jail."

"Just like that?" Dana was surprised.

"Just like that. Bev was pregnant with Ollie at the time. She divorced him six months later." He spoke mechanically as if speaking with emotion would make his part in the girls' neglect that much more heinous.

"Do guilty people do that?"

"What?"

"Plead guilty." She frowned.

"What do you mean?" Brady sat up.

"It seems as if the people who are guilty always plead not guilty and get really good lawyers who get them off."

"What are you saying?"

"Nothing. I don't know anything about your brother's case. All I know is that it seems strange for him to take a plea."

"You obviously haven't been around the justice system much. People plea-bargain all the time. After all, it's a lesser sentence. He's doing fifteen instead of twenty or thirty."

"But he's given up his whole life."

"Dana, he's a criminal. That's what happens to criminals who get caught. Don't believe him just because you want to."

She shook her head. "No. I mean, could he be protecting someone? He could have pled guilty rather than—"

"Impossible." Brady turned away from her. "Dana, I understand your need to see the good in everything. But in this case, put your sympathy toward the girls. Carson embezzled and got caught. He was getting generous kickbacks for laundering money through the company and it wasn't enough, so he started to alter the books."

"But why? Didn't you say he was successful? Why would he risk everything?"

"Dana, if you don't mind, I've given up on this particular problem. I don't know why he'd need money enough to do what he did."

"Don't you think you can figure it out? Isn't that your job? Don't you think that Carson deserves that?"

"He's in prison, he doesn't deserve much."

Dana recoiled from the contempt in his voice. "You can't believe that."

The look he gave her was very different from any other she'd seen in the past two days. The coldness was shocking. This was a man who didn't forgive easily—or maybe at all.

"You have no idea what I believe."

Dana closed her mouth. The conversation was over. Brady had settled back down on the couch to stare intently at a penguin waddling across an ice floe. She stretched her lips into a feeble smile. "I guess I'll take my stuff and go to bed." She stood to leave and as she turned, he put his hand on her arm.

"I'm sorry, Dana," Brady said, his voice quiet. "You just pushed a couple of buttons. You haven't said anything I haven't spent the past five years going over and over in my mind. It's no excuse for snapping at you."

"You didn't snap. And it's really none of my business." She was having difficulty ignoring the feel of his thumb as it rubbed against her pulse.

He gave her a ghost of a smile. "I think those three little girls make it your business. And you're probably right about Carson, but I can't deal with it now. I just want to get married and get custody of the girls."

Dana stayed silent, more uncertain about Brady than she'd been since she'd met him. She'd glimpsed that he was forward moving, come hell or high water, but he also was unforgiving. That bothered her.

She removed her hand from his and said softly, "Good night."

THE NEXT DAY after breakfast, Dana and the girls walked over to the school, the mood sober. Dana met the parents of her other students and they all asked in hushed tones if what they'd heard was true. Dana gave them only the briefest amount of information, assuring the parents that the girls were fine and that school would continue. She didn't tell them about her upcoming wedding, though.

It was a rough day. If her other students noticed how tired she was, they didn't comment. Dana hadn't been able to sleep after her discussion with Brady. After a half hour of tossing and turning, she got up, pulled on her robe and tried to focus her blurry eyes on the papers she needed to grade.

She'd finished all her papers and then started on her lesson plans. As dawn started to break, she was putting the final touches on the last lesson. It had been too late to sleep, too early to get up, so Dana had just lain there, looking for some sort of sign that she was doing the right thing. When Ollie and Jean had crept into her room, climbed into her bed and snuggled against her, she'd known she couldn't deny these girls a home.

Now it was the end of the long and arduous day. The older children were reading aloud, giving Dana the opportunity to observe the Moore girls. Ollie and Jean seemed to have returned to themselves. But Karen, usually a diligent student, hadn't been able to concentrate all day. Instead of following along in her book, Karen was staring outside, her young face pinched. Dana wondered if she should have given them the week off. On the other hand, if Karen wasn't here, she'd probably be brooding in bed.

The sound of tires crunching on the gravel came from the courtyard. Dana marked the spot in her book and said, "Okay, guys. You can go get your backpacks. Fifth grade—you have a test in English tomorrow. Third, second and first grades—you have spelling."

The kids nodded and started gathering their things.

When they were finished, they put their chairs up on their desks and ran outside to wait for their parents. Dana followed them out noting at once that Karen had perched on top of the picnic table. One by one, the parents claimed their children. As Dana discussed homework or student progress, she was upset to see Ollie and Jean had joined Karen. It was as if they were still expecting to see their mother's car. Fifteen minutes passed before the last parent left and the school grounds became quiet.

Dana sighed and glanced at her watch. How long should she let them wait before reminding them that their mother was dead? She walked over to the table.

"Hey, there," she greeted them.

Karen didn't look up, but Ollie smiled at her and gave a small wave of her fingers.

Dana waved back and tilted her head. "How are you doing?"

"Okay," was Karen's muffled answer.

Dana sat down on the bench. "How are you, Jean?"

Jean just stared at her, eyes wide.

Ollie tapped Dana on the shoulder. "Is Momma going to come to get us?"

Dana shook her head. "No."

"Sometimes she's late." Ollie sounded as if she was repeating something she'd heard Karen say many times before. "She'll be here any minute."

Dana shook her head. "I'm sorry, Ollie. She won't be coming."

"What do you mean?" Ollie tilted her head in an effort to understand. "Momma's coming back."

"No, honey. Your momma's gone to heaven."

Ollie wrinkled her nose. "Momma was sleeping. That's all."

"Momma's *not* sleeping," Karen snapped. "Momma's *dead!*" Karen choked back a sob.

Dana was at a loss for words. She knew exactly how Karen felt. She understood the pain of a broken heart and knew that no kindness ever really fixed it.

"Why did she do it, Miss Ritchie? Didn't she love us?" How unfair. Karen was trying so hard to understand the adult world, and that made Dana angry. Why had this eleven-year-old never had a childhood?

"She *did* love you. But she was sick and that's why she couldn't stop herself from doing what she did," Dana said, and unwillingly, she understood. She'd been through this before. Adam's image appeared before her as if she was watching the opening scene of a movie in a theater.

"What are you doing?"

Adam pushed his stubby fingers through his black hair, making it spiky. "Nothing."

"You must be doing something." Dana came

up to investigate. In a grubby plastic water bottle Adam had placed a dandelion. "That's very nice. But are you sure you want to put it by the door? You can put it inside so you could see it."

He shook his head. "No. It's got to be here."

"Why?"

"Mom said to have a flower for her. A flower by the door means that you love someone."

Dana pinched her lips together. She'd spent five years filling out forms so she wouldn't have to think about Adam. Why was it now, after all this time, that he seemed so real she could touch him? Dana pushed thoughts of Adam away and held out her hands to Ollie and Jean. "Come on. Let's play."

"Miss Ritchie!" Ollie exclaimed. "Aren't you too old to play?"

Play. What was it like to play? To run around with an abandon that made one forget that the world was filled with hurt, anger and sorrow.

She smiled at Ollie, "No, I'm not. So what do you want to play?" She started walking backward away from the picnic table, pulling the girls with her.

Ollie and Jean looked at each other. "Line tag!" they cried in unison.

"Will your sister play, too?" Dana asked,

watching Karen, who was wiping her eyes on her sleeve.

"Karen, come play," Ollie begged.

Karen shook her head. "No. I don't feel like it."

"Please, Karen?"

"No," Karen said sharply, quelling much of her sisters' enthusiasm. But Ollie and Jean still allowed Dana to lead them to the playground that was filled with so many different lines—from bright yellow to faded white—that they had to discuss which ones counted.

"All of them!" Ollie declared. Jean nodded her agreement.

That was easy. "So should I be it?" Dana asked with a smile.

"You need to give us a head start," Jean pointed out.

"'Cause you're bigger," Ollie explained.

Dana nodded her understanding. "I'll count to ten."

"Count to one hundred!" Ollie screamed as she started running.

"I'll count to twenty," Dana compromised. "Should I cover my eyes?"

"Yes!" Both girls giggled.

Dana closed her eyes and began counting at a

slow deliberate pace. "...Nineteen, nineteen and a half, nineteen and three-quarters...twenty!" She opened her eyes and found that Jean and Ollie were on either side of the playground.

Dana took a deep breath and, being very careful to stay on the lines, began to run. She could feel her heartbeat accelerate; she heard her ankles pop. She chased after Jean first and the little girl screamed with glee. After a moment Dana changed direction and began to pursue Ollie who'd strayed a little too close. Back and forth she went until she had to stop to catch her breath. Looking up, she noticed that Karen was watching them rather than the road.

She waved Karen over. "I need someone on *my* side. These two are too fast for me!"

Karen hesitated, and then with great reluctance, put her backpack aside and climbed off the table. Without warning, she dashed onto the playground, running after Ollie who screeched with laughter. Somehow, someway, they all ended up in the same place at the same time. Dana tried to keep her balance, but couldn't. Resigned, she let herself plop onto the ground. When was the last time she'd lain on the ground and looked up at the sky? It had been a long time. *Too* long. She heard Karen laughing and thought it was worth being here with gravel poking at the back of her neck to hear Karen's mirth.

"Momma used to do that with us."

Dana turned her head to look at the girl. "What?"

"Play. She used to be fun."

"What happened?"

Karen shrugged. "We had to move real quick."

"That must have been hard." Dana didn't want to know the circumstances that had made them move so quickly.

"I didn't get my ears pierced."

"What?" Dana didn't follow Karen's abrupt change in subject.

"I was supposed to get my ears pierced with my friend in Hollister. She and her mom were going to come pick me up, but Momma said we had to move that day and that she'd make it up to me. I still don't have my ears pierced, though." Karen's eyes welled up again. "I guess I won't be able to now."

Dana sat up and pulled Karen into her lap, vowing to try to give Karen a childhood.

BRADY TIGHTENED THE LAST SCREW on the new chain he was putting on Dana's front door. He'd heard Dana and the girls laughing before and wondered what they were doing now. As he cleaned up his tools he was struck by how much Dana had changed in just three days. On Friday it had seemed as if she could barely stand to have them in her house. Now she looked like their mother. His heart thumped. He didn't have to marry her to get her to care for these girls, she'd cared for them almost instantly.

The noise they made caused him to stand up.

At first, she looked as if she was crying, but as he started to go and help her, he realized that she was laughing. Ollie, Jean and Karen were laughing, too. He wasn't sure what was so funny, but he felt left out. He wanted to laugh like that…with her. However, after snapping at her the night before, he wasn't sure that Dana would want to laugh with him. Before he knew what he was doing, he was striding across the parking lot to the playground.

Dana looked up when his shadow passed over them.

"Hi," Brady said.

"Hi, Uncle Brady!" Ollie waved at him.

With two arms, he swooped down and plucked Jean and Ollie off Dana. "Hi, Ollie and Jean. Or is it Jean and Ollie?"

"*I'm* Ollie," Ollie said indignantly. She pointed to Jean. "That's Jean."

"*I'm* Jean!" Jean shouted and then looked abashed.

"No, I think you're Penelope," Brady said with a wink to Karen, who had stood up and was brushing herself off.

"I'm not Pe-nel-o-pie," Jean protested. "I'm Jean."

"Hmm. Then who's Penelope?"

"There is no Penelope," Ollie guessed.

"Poor Penelope." He looked down at Dana. "Maybe she's Penelope."

"That's Miss Ritchie."

Still on the ground, Dana was smiling at his silly conversation, and he was glad. He put down the girls, and Dana said, "I'm sure there's cartoons on."

Even Karen perked up at the thought of cartoons. She started to run to the house and then stopped, looking at the table where their backpacks were.

"I'll get them," Dana called. "You go in and watch television."

With just the briefest of hesitations, Karen followed her sisters. Dana raised herself up on her elbows, and he put his hand out. "Need help getting up?"

She grasped his hand. "Thank you," she said, letting him haul her up. Brady couldn't stop looking at her, and Dana started to fidget.

"What?" she demanded. "Is there dirt on my face?"

Brady shook his head, not understanding the feelings that were washing through him. Was it tenderness? He hadn't felt that for a long time. Not since he'd held his mother's hand on the day she died. Brady could barely speak. He cleared his throat and muttered, "You look fine."

"Then what are you staring at?"

"You should wear your hair down more often."

"W-what?" Dana stammered.

"You have beautiful hair," he repeated.

"This mousy-brown stuff?" Dana gave a nervous laugh. "It's the bane of my existence."

"It's got beautiful flecks of gold in it," he observed, capturing a strand.

"I'm sure you say that to all your spinster schoolteachers," Dana joked.

"No, just you," Brady said. And he couldn't have meant it more.

CHAPTER EIGHT

TO MEET BRADY'S GAZE took every ounce of courage that Dana possessed. He was serious and in his eyes was an intensity she'd never seen before. She bit her lip, wondering what she'd done to make him look at her that way. She *liked* the fact that he was doing it, wanted to encourage him. But how?

"I should—" She began to inch back as his smile changed from affectionate to something deeper, something scarier. She gestured toward the girls' backpacks on the picnic table.

"Don't go," he said, catching the edge of her blouse and tugging her back to him.

"I'm not going anywhere. I'm just going to pick up the girls' stuff."

"We need to talk."

"Talk?" Her mind was whirling. What could he want to talk about?

"I've got the M.E.'s report on Bev."

Dana felt an acute sense of disappointment. Of

course he would want to tell her about Bev when the children weren't around. What was she thinking? That he wanted to talk about personal feelings? About his brother?

"What have you heard?" she asked, her smile fading.

"It's definitely a suicide. She died in the car after taking a lot of different pills."

Dana felt a knot form in the pit of her stomach. She kicked at a piece of gravel and watched it travel three or four yards. "Those poor girls."

"That's an understatement."

"So what happens now? Is temporary custody ours?"

"If it's still the two of us, it is," Brady said.

There was a long pause. Dana nodded. "Yes. It's still the two of us. We can do it together."

Dana didn't know what to think when Brady grabbed her and pulled her against him in a big bear hug.

ONE MINUTE BRADY was hugging Dana in a friendly way. Then, as she slid down his chest, it changed into something more intimate. She stared up at him and repeated, "Together."

Whether it was her breathy tone or the luminescence of her brown eyes, which seemed to swallow him, the word sounded like a pact that needed to be sealed. Without even thinking about any of the consequences, Brady slowly bent his head and pressed his lips to hers. Her muffled "oh" had him pulling her closer. He wasn't aware of the shapeless brown skirt, but rather the very attractive curves beneath. It was only supposed to be a simple kiss to seal their bargain, but when her arms went around his neck, he couldn't do anything but sink deeper into the kiss.

"Miss Ritchie?" a small voice startled them both.

Dana jerked back so quickly that if Brady hadn't braced her, she would have fallen.

"Y-yes, Ollie?" Dana asked.

"Why are you kissing Uncle Brady?"

Blushing, Dana looked at Brady, as if she was hoping he had some snappy explanation. She smoothed back her hair and then her skirt.

"We were just practicing for when we get married on Friday," Brady answered.

Dana looked impressed. "Is there something you wanted, Ollie?" she prompted.

Ollie scrunched her forehead. "I forget." She turned to walk back to the house, then stopped and motioned to them. "Come with me."

"You guys go. I'll go get the backpacks," Dana said, waving them on.

Dana watched Brady lift Ollie, put her under his arm like a football and take off at a run. She closed her eyes. He had kissed her, really truly kissed her. And she had kissed him back. She picked up the backpacks and decided that one kiss wasn't enough. She'd only known the man for three days, yet she was kissing him as if they were on the verge of something more. It had her thinking that they might be able to make their arrangement permanent. Could they be a family? She wanted to believe it, but common sense told her differently.

Eventually Brady and the girls wouldn't need her. They would move into a nice house, make their own lives and that would be that. She hugged the three little backpacks to her chest and slowly walked back to the cottage. She had to be sensible and realistic about her marriage. It was definitely not forever.

As she entered the house, she noticed the shiny new bolt on the door. He'd said he would fix it and he had. He was a man of his word. That wasn't the only thing he'd done. The whole living room had been cleaned from top to bottom. The girls were on the floor, their eyes glued to the television set, drinking tall glasses of milk and eating apple slices from a large bowl. She recognized the bowl, but she knew she didn't have anything that resembled apples or milk in her fridge. They waved to her when she came into the room.

"I think it's time for homework," she suggested.

Karen looked up. "But you have it," she said with perfect kid logic.

"You're right. But now that your homework's here, the television goes off." She deposited their backpacks next to them and turned off the television. Once she saw that the girls were happy to comply, she went into the kitchen where Brady was pulling out beautiful vegetables from the refrigerator.

"I see you did some shopping," she observed, leaning against the counter.

"You were at school all day." He shrugged. "It didn't make sense to wait for you. Plus, we needed lunch things for the girls this week. I bought enough to last until the weekend."

"So what's for dinner, honey?" Dana joked.

"Chicken with some veggies," he replied, rinsing both green and red bell peppers with his capable hands. He glanced over his shoulder at her. "Can you get me a few carrots?"

Dana obliged, opening the refrigerator door to see a ten-pound bag of carrots on the bottom shelf. "How many?"

"Four or five."

She pulled out the requisite carrots and handed them to him. "You know," she said, "I didn't expect you to clean up the place. I'm embarrassed."

"Don't be. There's a lot of work when five people live in one house. I put the laundry that was in the dryer on your bed. I wanted to get more of the girls' things done."

"Laundry, too?" Her eyes went wide. "So you cook, you clean, you do laundry, you fix locks, and you protect the public. Is there anything else I should know about you?"

He grinned. "I'm a nice guy."

"I'm sure you are."

"And he's a good kisser," Ollie called.

"How do you know that?" Karen asked.

"He was kissing Miss Ritchie."

Karen looked at them speculatively, "Really? Isn't that supposed to wait until after you're married?"

"Is kissing what gives you babies?" Ollie asked.

"No, silly. Kissing doesn't give you a baby," Karen said with older-sister scorn.

"So what does?"

Brady pretended not to hear. Dana stood quickly. "You have to be in love to have a baby, Ollie. I'm going to change and then I need to go back to the school and get some work done."

"Can I go, too?" Ollie asked.

"No," Brady answered for her. "Miss Ritchie is going to be busy and you have homework. In a little bit you can all help me cook dinner. Dana?"

"Yes?"

"Dinner will be at six-thirty. Please be sure that you're on time." He gave her a smile that made her heart sing.

"I'll try."

"Don't try. Just be here."

Just be here. Seemed like a simple idea. But as she glanced up at the clock and realized she still had about an hour's worth of work and a half hour to complete it, she knew it wasn't. For years she'd answered to no one's schedule but her own. If she wanted bacon and eggs for dinner, that's what she had. Curiously though, she wasn't upset by her loss of freedom. It felt good to know she had a family to go home to. She put her head down and worked on the forms. She didn't want to leave her family again tonight.

At twenty past, Jean came running over to tell her it was time for dinner. And as they walked back to the house, Jean slipped her hand in Dana's. It felt so good, so natural to have that small hand in hers.

The dinner table was beautifully set and the kitchen was filled with wonderful aromas. Brady pulled out her chair, and they all sat down to their first family dinner.

This was what it was like, she realized. She'd been so busy avoiding the pain that loving brought that she'd missed out on the joy. What a terrible mistake.

After dinner was finished and the girls were bathed, they all watched television for an hour, Dana and Brady on either end of the couch, the three girls between them. By the time the program was over, Ollie had crawled into Dana's lap and Jean had curled up against Brady. In sync with Brady, she stood and then together they got the girls to bed.

After the girls were tucked in, Dana and Brady went back to the couch. Without the girls as a buffer, Dana felt like a teenager. She wanted him to kiss her, but instead they watched another comedy, before he switched to a newsmagazine show.

At the first commercial break, he muted the sound and said, "The coroner will be releasing Bev's body on Thursday. I'll take the girls to see her after school then."

"Thank you." She really was grateful. Though she knew it was important for the girls, especially Karen, to see their mother, Dana didn't want to see Bev.

The show came back on but Brady didn't turn up the sound. "I made an appointment with the judge on Friday at four."

"Oh." Dana curled her legs up under her.

"Not nervous, are you?" Brady's eyes were sympathetic.

"Very." She searched his face, her heart beating at twice its normal rate. "Are we doing the right thing?"

Brady looked in the direction of the girls' room. "Yes." His voice was sure. "For those three reasons in there."

Dana nodded, not sure what to say next.

"I'm sorry," he apologized, resting his hand on her bare forearm.

"For what?" Dana felt a thousand goose

bumps form in the wake of Brady's rhythmic stroke.

"I doubt this is going to be the wedding ceremony you've dreamed of."

She smiled. "It's probably not the kind of marriage I've dreamed of either."

"We'll make it work." Brady was earnest. "We have every reason in the world to make it work. I'm not the easiest person to get to know—"

She laughed. "How can you say that to the most reclusive woman in the Central Valley?"

Brady took a deep breath. "Maybe that's why this will work. I hope I can get this family stuff right."

"After the cleaning, the dinner and the bedtime stories, you must be joking," Dana said. "You do it like a pro. Why haven't you married?" The words popped out of her mouth before she could stop them. "I'm sorry. It's none of my business."

Brady shook his head. "That's not true. Most everything about me is about to become your business. The sad fact is I never met the right woman."

"You still haven't, but you're going to marry me."

"I think you're the right woman. And every

hour that I know you, I become more convinced that I couldn't ask for anyone more suitable.''

Dana wasn't sure that was a compliment, but his stroking had turned her brain to mush.

''Have you thought about what you're going to wear?'' Brady asked suddenly.

''No.'' What did you wear to an impromptu wedding?

Brady pulled a crumpled wad of bills from his pocket and gave it to her.

She stared at it. ''What's this for?''

''Maybe after school tomorrow you can go shopping for dresses for you and the girls. Something nice to mark the occasion.''

She tried to make him take the money back. ''I can buy us dresses.''

He shook his head and reached out to touch her cheek. ''Please, let me. As my wedding present to you.'' Brady tangled his fingers in her hair and gently nudged her close so that he could give her a long, not-so-chaste kiss. Dana closed her eyes. This kiss was different from the kiss on the playground. This one was passion from start to finish.

It was easy to go farther. As he pushed her back against the couch, she felt her body molding against the warmth of his chest and legs. With a deep groan, he wrenched himself away.

"Sorry," she whispered. "I've scared you away."

He shook his head. "I'm afraid of scaring you away."

"I'm still here."

He gave her a teasing smile. "You'd better go to bed. Or we couldn't even begin to think about an annulment."

"You know we have to start thinking beyond Friday," Dana said in a rush.

"What do you mean?"

"You can't sleep on the couch forever."

"Short of making the girls sleep on the couch, I don't see what other alternative there is."

After that kiss, he could say that? Dana didn't know whether she should be pleased or insulted. "You can always stay with me."

"You should go to sleep while you can," he replied.

With a nod of assent, Dana stood up and hurried down the hall, his wad of bills clutched in her hands. Once in the safety of her bedroom, she leaned back against the door. Then she remembered something that she'd forgotten. She was getting married and hadn't told her parents.

"You're what?" her mother squeaked as soon as Dana told her.

"I'm getting married on Friday, Mom. Just wanted you and Dad to know." Dana lay on her bed, staring at her ceiling fixture.

"To who? Do we know him?"

"No. I didn't know him until last week."

"Last week? Harold, wake up, your daughter's getting married on Friday to a man she met last week."

"Congratulations, honey," Dana could hear her father say drowsily in the background.

"What does he do?"

"He's a deputy sheriff for the county." Dana hesitated. "There's more."

"More?"

"Yes. There are three little girls."

"The ones that were left with you on Friday?" Her mother's tone was laced with concern.

"Yes," she admitted. "Those little girls."

"Oh, Dana, not again." Her mother's frustration was born of love. "I remember how awful it was for you when—"

"Their mother committed suicide, so we're going to make a family, Mom. The deputy—Brady—is their uncle. He can't get custody by himself. He needs me." The reason sounded so weak when she said it out loud.

"But this is how you get hurt."

"I know, Mom." Dana felt her eyes fill with tears. "But you should see these little girls. *They* need me."

"And you need them?"

Dana stared at the phone, amazed at her mother's insight. She nodded even though her mother couldn't see her. "Yes, Mom. I need them."

"Do you love him?"

"No." Dana was reasonably sure she was telling the truth.

"Can you grow to love him?"

"Yes." Her affirmation was so soft she barely heard it herself.

AFTER SCHOOL THE NEXT DAY, Dana put the girls into the back of her car and drove to Los Banos to see if she could find them dresses for Friday. The prospect of a trip to town seemed to excite the little girls. At Wal-Mart, Dana shot out of the car and hustled the three girls inside. As if she'd been doing it for years, Dana pulled out a cart, plopped Ollie in the seat and headed for the children's section, with Jean and Karen hanging on to either side.

The girls were overwhelmed by the choices they had. They hung back, unwilling to stray far from Dana. She, however, was on a mission. With no ceremony, underwear, socks, T-shirts and even hair ribbons began to pile up in the cart.

That chore done, Dana pushed the cart over to the dresses. "Which one do you like?" Dana asked. She pulled out a pink dress decorated with little rosebuds and held it up to Jean. "Do you like this?"

"Pretty," Jean said, nodding her head.

"Do you want to look alike? Or do you want to wear different dresses?"

"Whatever you think is best," Karen whispered deferentially.

"Karen, I'm not going to be wearing the dress." Dana smiled. "You are. So we should find something that you really, really like."

Ollie reached out of the cart and plucked at the rosebud dress. "I like this one."

Dana shuffled through the rack looking for one in Ollie's size. "Here." She lifted Ollie out of the cart and held the dress up to her. "You both are going to look so cute." She fished in the cart and pulled out a package of hair ribbons and put it next to the dresses. "Perfect!"

Jean and Ollie clapped, big smiles on their faces.

When Dana looked up, she noticed that Karen had wandered to the other side of the rack. She fingered the material of a dress and then looked at the price tag. She moved on to another dress and looked at the tag. Finally, she found one and pulled it out.

"This one's on sale," Karen said.

Dana looked at the dress, a drab gray, more sober than any of the ones surrounding it. "Do you like it?" she asked.

"It's on sale." Karen looked hopeful.

"We don't have to buy dresses that are on sale. This time we're going to buy dresses that we like. So do you like it?"

Karen scrunched her face. "I don't know."

Dana went around and picked out the first dress Karen had looked at. "Do you like it better than this one?"

Karen shook her head.

"Why don't you go try this one on. To see if it fits." Dana grabbed three more dresses and gave them to Karen. "Why don't you try these on, too."

"All of them?" Karen's eyes were big. "These are really expensive."

"Well, we're not going to buy all of them, just your favorite. We'll wait out here for you."

Karen disappeared into the cubicle of a dressing room. When Jean got tired of standing, Dana made room for her in the cart.

Ten minutes later, Karen came back out, her eyes shining.

"Have you decided?"

She shyly handed the dress of choice to Dana. It was a beautiful dress in a pink floral chiffon. "I think these three dresses are going to go perfect with each other."

Karen hung on to the cart as they went down the aisle. "Now we need to find a dress for you!"

"Yes, we do, don't we?"

In the women's section Dana picked out a conservative peach dress.

Karen wrinkled her nose.

"No?"

Karen shook her head.

"Well, which one?"

"Something like this!" Karen pointed to a clingy white cotton lace dress that was only slightly more substantial than a slip. "It's got sparkles in it."

Dana hesitated. "You think?"

All three girls nodded.

Dana picked the hanger off the rack and held it up. "I've never worn anything like this before."

"It'll look real pretty on you," Karen assured her. "Go try it on."

So Dana did as she was told, taking all three

girls into the dressing room with her. The dress fit perfectly but Dana didn't know if she liked it. It was so short, so clingy, so...*flirty.*

"You should get that," Karen said with great confidence. "Uncle Brady will think you're pretty."

With a laugh, Dana decided to buy it. After an endorsement like that, how could she go wrong?

"Just shoes left to get," Dana said after she'd changed back into her own clothes. They scoured the shoe department trying on dozens of shoes. Ollie and Jean got matching shoes to coordinate with their rosebud dresses, and Karen chose a pretty pair of patent-leather Mary Janes. Dana found a pair of white heels, even though she knew she'd wear them only once. Heading toward the checkout, they came upon the jewelry counter.

"You need a ring for Uncle Brady," Karen reminded her.

Dana stopped. It hadn't occurred to her to get a ring for Brady, but if this was going to look real, he would need to have a ring.

"I don't know his ring size," Dana replied as her eyes scanned the wedding bands.

A much-pierced clerk leaned up against the case. She was chewing gum but her smile was genuine. "Are his hands bigger than yours?"

Dana nodded.

"If you get something that fits your thumb, it'll probably be pretty close. You can have it sized later."

"Get that one," Karen whispered, pointing to a simple white-gold band.

"I like it," Dana admitted.

"Try it to see if it fits your thumb."

The clerk brought it out and Dana slid the cool metal onto her thumb. She held it up for the girls to inspect. "Well, it fits."

"That's the one." Karen nodded.

"We do piercing, too." The clerk said with a gesture at Jean who had wandered over to the earring display.

"What?"

The clerk grinned at Karen. "We pierce ears."

Karen immediately started playing with her ears, and she looked at Dana with large, pleading eyes.

Dana hesitated. "I don't know... What do we have to do?"

"Just sign the parental consent form."

Dana hadn't forgotten what Karen had told her about her mother's promise. "Do you want to get your ears pierced?" Dana asked and then added, "With me?"

Karen nodded. "With you, especially."

"Me, too," Ollie said. "Me, too."

"Is she too young?" Dana asked the clerk.

The clerk shook her head. "Nope. I did a baby last night."

"Does it hurt?" Karen asked.

"Yes."

Dana made a face. Karen flinched, but then straightened her small back as the clerk started to walk over to the earring display.

"Dolphins!" Karen said. She looked up at Dana. "Can I have the dolphins?"

Dana wasn't sure what to do. In a matter of days, she and Brady would be married and have temporary custody of the children. It would be prudent to wait until after they had custody before poking holes in the girls' ears.

"Please?" Karen's gray eyes were shining with anticipation.

Dana made her decision. "Are you sure you want the dolphins? They have to be in your ears for a long time before you can change them. And you have to take very good care of them."

"I will. I want the dolphins."

"Okay, the dolphins for this one," Dana said.

As the clerk prepared the paperwork, Dana turned to Jean. "Do you want your ears pierced?"

Jean shook her head.

"I do!" Ollie said.

"Okay," Dana lifted Ollie into her arms and

indicated the array of studs. "Which ones do you want?"

Ollie squinched her eyes and then pointed to little pink crystal flowers.

"I like those."

"Here you go," the clerk said and put two forms in front of Dana. She filled them out and signed her name at the bottom. Then Karen got in the chair, and the clerk drew tiny dots on her ears. Dana and the clerk looked carefully to make sure the dots were centered. When they both agreed the marks were in the right place, the clerk leaned over Karen and pierced first her left ear, then her right.

"Did it hurt?" Ollie asked.

"Just for a little bit."

"Do you still want your ears done?" Dana asked.

Ollie nodded.

"Okay. She wants the flowers."

"Don't cry," Karen instructed Ollie. "It's going to hurt but don't cry."

And tough little trouper that she was, Ollie had her ears pierced without as much as a squeak.

"Now what about you, Jean. We have to get you something." Dana said as she put Ollie back in the cart. "What about a ring?" She lifted Jean into her arms and leaned over a case filled with birthstone rings. It was at that moment she realized that she had no idea when the girls' birthdays were. For that matter, she didn't know Brady's.

"February," whispered Karen. "Jean's birthday is in February."

Dana smiled and whispered back, "Thank you." Clearing her throat, she asked, "Can we see the February ring?"

"That's an amethyst," the clerk told them. "Do you know what amethyst does?"

They all shook their heads.

"It protects its wearer from bad spirits."

"Well, then, Miss Jean," Dana said. "I think this ring is just perfect for you. It will protect you in your dreams."

Jean took the ring that the clerk held out and put it on her finger. She looked at Dana in wonder. "It fits."

"We'll take that, too, along with the wedding band."

"Done. Anything else?"

Dana laughed. "No, I think we've done quite enough damage already."

As she paid, Karen sidled up next to her. "Don't tell Uncle Brady about his ring. Let it be a surprise."

CHAPTER NINE

BRADY HAD JUST FINISHED adding the final ingredients to his special hamburger surprise when the door burst open and the girls came in with their arms filled with packages.

"Uncle Brady!" Karen was the first one in the kitchen. "Look!" She angled her head to show him something.

"What?" He looked at her hair, but didn't know what he was supposed to see.

"My *ear*," she instructed him.

"I see your ear," he teased her.

"What's *on* the ear?" she asked.

"I see a little dolphin."

"Miss Ritchie let me and Ollie get our ears pierced! And we got the prettiest dresses for your wedding. And Miss Ritchie bought a pretty dress, too, but you can't see that until Friday."

"She did, did she?" Brady murmured.

Dana, her face red, grabbed the packages and headed to her room.

"Are you going to show me?" Brady called to her retreating back.

She stopped, turned and gave him a smile that could only be called saucy, before disappearing into her bedroom.

"Look," a small voice said to him.

Jean was tugging on his sleeve. Brady knelt down next to the little girl. "Did you get your ears pierced, too?"

Jean shook her head and held out her hand.

"Oh, you have a ring. It's very pretty."

"It's her birthstone," Karen informed him, looking into a spoon to catch the reflection of her ears.

"The clerk told us that the amethyst will protect Jean from bad spirits," Dana said when she came back into the room. She looked at the stove. "That smells good. I could get used to this."

"You've had quite a shopping trip." He gestured at the girls who were in the living room, admiring their new jewelry.

Guiltily Dana put her hands behind her back. "It's probably something we should have talked about. But yesterday Karen told me that her mom had promised she could get it done, because they had to move away from Hollister on the day she was supposed to have her ears pierced there.

When we realized they did piercing at the store, I couldn't resist. I did sign the parental consent form, though. Bad?''

"What did you say?"

"That I signed the consent form."

Brady shook his head. "No, before that. You said something about Bev moving away from Hollister."

"Karen said they moved away in a hurry. Is it important?"

"It might be. If we knew why she had to move so quickly, we might know why she'd want to hurt herself."

"Money?"

"Probably." In his experience, people did a lot of things for money. Many of them illegal. Carson was a case in point.

"Speaking of which, every penny you gave me is gone." She leaned over the counter and plucked a mushroom off the cutting board and popped it into her mouth. "Is it terrible that I had the girls' ears pierced?"

Brady had never wanted to kiss someone the way he wanted to kiss Dana right now. "No. Not bad at all. Look how happy they are. I'm surprised Jean didn't get her ears pierced, too."

"She knows her own mind," Dana replied with

true affection in her voice. "She knew from the very beginning she didn't want it. I'm very proud of them all."

The girls had stopped what they were doing when they heard Dana's praise. And the change it made in them was notable. Brady had read studies that proved how important unconditional love was to a child. And here was living proof. He didn't know how it had happened, but finally he was going to be able to do something he knew his mother would be proud of.

BRADY WAITED in front of the large oak desk in the judge's chambers, surprisingly nervous. In his suit pocket, he fingered the simple gold band he'd purchased the day before at a local jewelry store after he'd taken the girls to see their mother. Looking at them now he realized how proud he was of them. They knew their mother had been driven by her pain to do some bad thing, but they forgave her, letting go of any anger they might have had. Moments ago Karen had whispered to him that Dana was going to come in by herself and that he had to be surprised. He assured her he would act very surprised and stood up straighter when the judge entered the chambers.

The door opened, and with big smiles the girls

watched his expression as Dana came in. Teetering on high heels, she walked the short distance from the door to Brady, holding a small bunch of flowers that Jean and Ollie had picked that morning.

Brady discovered he didn't have to act surprised. He was stunned.

"Isn't she pretty, Uncle Brady?" Karen asked.

Pretty wasn't the word for it. He now knew why she'd wrapped herself up in a trench coat for the drive to Hollister.

"It's a bit excessive," she confessed.

"You're beautiful," were the only words he could come up with. He tried to find a less trite remark, but he was distracted by her gorgeous legs. He held out his hand and she placed her shaky one in it.

The ceremony took hardly any time at all, once the witnesses—two clerks Brady had found taking a break outside—arrived. Her hand only trembled slightly when he pushed the ring onto her finger. He hadn't expected her to have one for him, but found himself pleased by her thoughtfulness. After they signed their names on the marriage certificate, the judge reviewed the material for the temporary custody arrangement and granted it to them.

Once they were finally outside, Dana burst into nervous laughter.

"So what does this mean?" Karen asked.

"This means you three get to stay with us."

"Forever?"

"As much of forever as we can control," Brady said.

"Does that mean we have to call you Mom and Dad?" There was a quiver in Karen's voice.

Dana bent down. "No. You have a mother and a father. And they'll always be your mom and dad."

Karen looked relieved. "So I can call you Miss Ritchie and Uncle Brady?"

"That's fine."

"Or you can call her Aunt Dana," Brady suggested.

"Aunt Dana," Karen tried it, then nodded. "We'll call you Aunt Dana."

"So what do we want to do now?" Brady asked.

"I'm starving," Dana replied. "I've been so nervous, I haven't been able to eat all day."

"So where do we want to eat?" he said as he opened the car doors. When he helped Dana in, he found that she was still trembling.

"Thank you." She ducked her head shyly.

"Where do we want to eat?" he repeated when he got into the car.

"McDonald's!" Ollie said, clapping her little hands. "I like McDonald's."

Brady looked at Dana, who grinned. "If you go to the McDonald's by the county bank, they have a Playland."

THE GIRLS GOT LOUDER and louder once they saw the restaurant and couldn't get out of the car fast enough. Dana caught Ollie's hand to keep her from running across the parking lot. Not unhappy to be restrained, Ollie put her free hand in Brady's, then swung both arms. It seemed utter confirmation of the connection Dana now had with Brady and his nieces.

Dana had hardly recognized Brady in his nicely made gray suit. His hair was combed back and he'd shaved, revealing the straight planes of his face. This was a different Brady and he unnerved her. Especially when she remembered how he'd looked at her when she walked into the judge's chambers.

"What do you want?" Brady asked Dana, his voice close to her ear.

The fact that there was finally someone in her life who cared to know what she wanted made tears well up in Dana's eyes, but she fought them. She would not cry in a fast food restaurant.

"A burger? Nuggets?"

She pressed her lips tightly together and said, "A burger is fine."

"Fries?"

"A Happy Meal," Ollie said. "Get a Happy Meal."

Dana's tears spilled over. "Okay."

Brady glanced at Dana with concern. "Are you okay? Do you want to take this to go?"

She sniffled and clenched her hands into fists.

"Hey, you have quite a grip on that." He tugged her purse from her hand and gave it to Ollie. "You don't want to be accused of purse mangling on your wedding day."

"I'm sorry." The more she tried to hold back her tears, the worse the deluge became. She looked over her shoulder at the line forming behind her. Brady waved them past.

"Do you need a hankie?" he offered.

"You have a hankie?"

"No, but I've got a wad of toilet paper in my pocket." His words were joking but his eyes were serious. He pressed a tissue into her hand. Dana took a deep breath and Brady nodded approvingly.

"Is your meltdown over?" he teased.

Sure enough, more tears came.

"So is this where I'm supposed to hold you?"

She nodded. "Yes."

She closed her eyes as she felt his arms come around her with none of the reluctance that his tone suggested. She buried her face in his chest until she had no tears left.

"Make sure you use the toilet paper. This is my only clean shirt."

She was trying to cry but she felt a smile tug at the corners of her mouth. "Don't make me laugh."

Even though she wanted to stay in his arms forever, she reluctantly pulled away. She blew her nose in the tissue, straightened her shoulders and looked up at the menu. "I'm sorry. I really am happy."

"As you should be," Brady teased. "It is our wedding day. So enough of the waterworks. What do you want?"

Dana smiled down at Ollie. "A Happy Meal."

DANA WIPED the crumbs off the table in the booth she'd selected. She felt so much better now. Jean sat next to her and patted her leg.

"These are happy tears," she told the little girl.

Jean nodded and patted her leg some more. Brady walked toward them with the tray, and Karen and Ollie followed behind.

He put the tray on the table, and the girls scrambled into the booth, Karen scooting next to Dana. Brady passed out the Happy Meals, and the next few minutes were filled with chaos as the girls dug in the boxes for their toys.

Brady winked at her as he bit into his burger. Dana's heart fluttered. He was even handsome chewing. She watched him carefully tear open a package of ketchup for Ollie, and then one for Jean. Her appetite was still gone, and for some reason she couldn't take her eyes off him.

"Did you eat at McDonald's with the little boy?" Karen asked suddenly.

"What?" Dana didn't understand the question.

"I asked if you ate at McDonald's with the little boy."

"What little boy?" Suspicious of where this was going Dana couldn't keep a slight edge from creeping into her voice.

Karen paled. "I'm sorry. I saw the pictures of you and a little boy."

Dana swallowed as Adam's face rose in front of her. *Don't forget me.*

BRADY SAW DANA'S FACE go white. She didn't answer Karen for a long time. Instead, she focused on the fry that she was swirling around in a blob of ketchup that had already begun to crust.

"Where did you see those pictures?" Her voice was calm.

"In our room."

"Those pictures weren't out."

"I like photo albums." There was an apologetic tone in Karen's voice. "I saw them in the bookshelf and I started looking through them. I didn't mean to be bad. But there are lots and lots of pictures of him. He looks very nice. Where is he?"

Brady stared at Dana with concern. He didn't want to think about who this little boy was.

"What was his name?" Ollie asked.

"Dana, you don't have to answer that," Brady intervened. "Ollie, that's none of our business."

Ollie looked down. Her bottom lip trembled and tears started to run down her face. "I'm sorry."

"Adam," Dana said, her voice so low that Brady could barely hear her.

"What?"

"Adam." Dana spoke to Karen and Ollie.

"The little boy in the pictures is, was, named Adam."

"Was?" Brady asked.

"He died not long after those pictures were taken."

"Died?" Karen asked quietly. "Was he your baby?"

Dana locked her eyes on Brady's. "No. He was a student of mine. I took care of him for a summer while his mother was going through a tough time."

Brady understood Dana's inference. Tough times could mean drugs, violence or both. From the pain he saw on Dana's face, he could only imagine what the little boy had suffered before he went into Dana's care.

"How did he die?" Karen's voice had lowered to a whisper.

"His mother— He was in an accident," Dana amended. "Nothing could have saved him."

Dana was saying one thing but her posture said something different. Knowing Dana, she'd tried to do all that she could and failed. More likely, the system had failed. Too late, he realized what caring for his nieces must have cost her.

"We can't save everyone." The words came

out sounding much more stale than he intended.
Dana lifted her eyes to him.

"I wonder." She contemplated his words, and
with a resolve that startled him, Dana smiled.
"Hey, when we finish eating, why don't we get
ice cream, too. After all, we have to celebrate."

MUCH LATER when the girls were tucked into bed,
Dana sat at the kitchen table while Brady watched
television. She had a stack of homework to grade,
but she couldn't concentrate. She kept getting distracted by the thought of being married and wondering if she felt any different. She glanced over
at Brady who had changed out of his suit into
jeans and a T-shirt. His fingers tapped against the
remote.

"Anything interesting on?"

Brady glanced up. "No."

If she hadn't known better, she would have said
he was nervous.

Dana smiled. Today, they'd become a family.
It's not a real family, her rational mind tried to
tell her. She shook it off. *He's my husband.
They're my girls.* Despite all the warnings she'd
given herself, she'd been repeating those phrases
to herself and they sounded right.

"I'm not finding anything. Maybe you can," Brady said, and held up the remote.

She got up and crossed over to the living room. She settled down beside him and began to channel surf. She was sitting on her own couch watching her own TV in her own house. Why did she feel so odd?

"You looked great, today," Brady said after she started her second lap through the channels.

She stared at her fingers. "Thanks. The girls picked out the dress. I don't think I would have chosen it. When I tried it on this morning, I was shocked by how short it was, hence the coat."

"I'm glad you took off the coat. Not that you didn't look good in the coat, but you looked better in the dress."

"You didn't look so bad yourself."

"It may not have been a traditional wedding," he replied thoughtfully, "but I think that any wedding, especially ours, deserves special attention."

"Happy Meals?" she chuckled.

"Very special."

Dana became very still, realizing that Brady was leaning closer to her. He put out a finger and traced her profile, starting with the top of her forehead. Every nerve in Dana's body was jumping once he started to trace around her lips. After a few minutes he slid his hand behind her head and began to massage her neck. Tension evaporated, and she actually moaned.

He smiled and shifted to place his lips on hers. Dana closed her eyes, her lips seeking greater contact with his. She lifted her arms and he pulled her onto his lap, but then he stopped.

"What?" Dana asked.

"How much, uh, experience have you had?" The question came out baldly.

"Define experience." Dana was wary.

"Boyfriends."

"One or two."

"One or two?" Brady raised an eyebrow.

"Okay, one and it didn't last that long."

"So you're a virgin."

Dana winced and scooted away. "Well, not technically, if that makes you feel better. Is that something I should have told you before the ceremony?"

"Yes. No. Uh, probably."

"Is it a problem?"

"No." His voice was gruff. "Not at all. I just assumed you had more experience."

"I guess I can go get some experience," she said, half rising from the couch. "I'll be right back. How far is it to the nearest pick-up bar?"

Brady laughed, caught her wrist and pulled her back onto his lap.

"I think not." Brady's eyes were intent. "Can I ask you a personal question?"

She nodded, knowing what he was going to ask. Was she a virgin out of choice or circumstance? She was probably both, since she believed that the choices people made led to their circumstances. She'd rehearsed the conversation in her mind, so she didn't appear to be unwanted goods.

"Who was he?"

"Who was who? My boyfriend?"

"The boy."

"I told you." Her voice stuck in her throat. "He was a student at the school that I worked at."

"Was that all he was?"

She turned away, her lips pressed tightly together. "I don't talk about Adam."

"MAYBE IT'S TIME you did." Brady tried to keep his voice gentle. He saw Dana struggle with her thoughts.

"I'm sorry." She shook her head, trying to get a grip on herself. "I haven't talked about Adam to anyone except my mother."

"Try me," he told her, remembering the words

that she'd whispered to Jean. "I'm right here with you."

"Adam," she began, and then wiped away the tears that had slipped down her cheeks. "Adam was six and a student in another class. His mother was a crack addict. The week before school let out for the summer, I went to work early and found him sleeping underneath one of the portables."

Brady kept his expression blank. He was afraid that if he let his anger show, she'd stop telling him what happened.

"I took him to the principal's office, and he wouldn't let go of my hand." She swallowed. "The school called the authorities and they sent a social worker out. She was up to her eyeballs in cases, and though I'm not sure how it happened, I volunteered to take him. He was a lot like Jean. Didn't talk much, didn't trust anyone but me. He slept with me the first three nights, clinging to me as if he was afraid I'd disappear and leave him alone."

"Did they find his mother?"

Dana nodded. "She went into rehab, and I took Adam to see her while she was there. I knew he wasn't my child. I *knew* it. I had no plans to adopt him. I just wanted to give him a safe place where he could be a child.'' She pressed her hand to her mouth.

''You don't have to do this. I shouldn't have asked you to.''

Dana shook her head. ''We had a terrific summer. We went to the beach, the amusement park. We hung out on the porch and he learned to read. He gained weight and started to grow. He'd been so undernourished that he was small for his age.'' She gave him a watery smile. ''He loved fruit of any kind. Apples, cantaloupe, watermelon, grapes—even the kind with seeds. He'd swallow those, too.''

Dana lapsed into silence.

''Then?'' Brady prompted.

''Then his mother got released and he was given back to her.''

''But you knew that would happen.''

''Yes, I did, and even though I loved him, I knew that she was his mother. But it was still the most difficult thing I've ever done.''

''But it didn't end there. You said he died.''

''He was killed.'' Dana's face twisted in pain. ''Two days later, his mother started using again. She called me and then while I listened she *shot* him and herself. I didn't know where she lived and I could hear Adam crying. Her aim wasn't that great and she only wounded him. By the time the police were able to trace the call, he was dead.'' Her story told, Dana broke down completely.

Brady closed his eyes and pulled her close.

''I don't know w-what else I could have done. I had to help him, but it hurt so much to lose him.''

''You did the right thing. You couldn't have done anything differently.''

''I don't honestly know anymore. But right or wrong, I'm living with the decision I made. I knew I couldn't teach there again, so I applied for this job. It's ideal. Far too much work for one person, which means I don't have to think and can't get involved. But what about now?'' She smiled helplessly. ''I think I've just done the same thing again.''

''Except for one big difference.'' Brady's voice was deep with the emotions he could feel emanate from her.

''What?''

''This time you're not doing it alone.''

CHAPTER TEN

BRADY'S WORDS SEEPED into Dana's subconscious like warm water. She turned to him and he put his arms around her. The ache that she'd managed to control for so many years, had somehow gotten free, finding release in the magic of a child's laugh and the tenderness of a strong man. Brady's arms tightened around her and she buried her face into him.

"For a business arrangement, this marriage feels awfully real," Dana said.

"I know." His voice rumbled against her ear.

"How can that be?"

"I don't know."

"The longer we're married, the harder it will be to consider an annulment." There, she'd said it.

"You're right." She could feel his lips on her temple.

"The paperwork would be a mess," she added.

"I know."

"What's keeping us from taking a shot at a real marriage? At a real family."

He pulled back to look at her. "The annulment was for you. I didn't want you to be tied to us, if you didn't want to be. I appreciate all that you've done for us and I wouldn't force you to stay longer than you wanted."

"I said the word *forever* today."

"You wouldn't be the first to take it back. Everyone would understand."

"But it's too late," Dana whispered.

"Too late?"

"I'm hooked. I don't want to give you, any of you, up."

She rose from the couch and held out her hand. He stared at it for a long time. She watched as the battle he fought with his emotions was played out on his face. Passion seemed to be winning, causing Dana to duck her head shyly, though she still kept her hand extended.

"Unless you'd like to wait until I get more experience," she said with a sly smile, "I'd like some time alone with my husband."

"Dana." He could barely say her name. "You need to think this through—"

"More than I did when I agreed to marry you?" She tilted her head.

Brady grasped her hand and let her pull him up. He stood only inches from her. "You need to be absolutely sure. And I don't mind waiting until you know me better."

"How much better am I supposed to know you?" She felt as if she could barely breathe. "I know you were willing to get married to save three little girls. I know you can cook, you can fix chains on doors, you can tell a mean bedtime story and you're a darned good kisser. What else is there?"

He appeared undecided. So she stood on her toes, wrapped her hands around his neck and kissed him.

"Dana," he groaned.

"Don't tell me you're afraid of a virgin?" she teased.

He shook his head and then admitted. "Yes."

"Don't be. I've read my share of women's magazines."

"It should be special. The first time," he muttered.

"And what's more special than your wedding night?" She balanced herself on the tips of her toes, relishing the heat emanating from his chest.

"Nothing," Brady whispered in her ear. With

a swoop, he hooked his arm around her legs and lifted her up.

Dana laughed in surprise, "What are you doing?"

"Carrying you over the threshold," he said as he walked down the hall. At the bedroom door, he asked again, "Are you sure?"

She stared into his eyes, her heart in her throat. "More sure than I've ever been."

He pushed open the door with his shoulder.

THE NEXT MORNING, they were awakened by three children creeping up next to the bed. Brady opened one eye to see Jean's nose a fraction of an inch from his.

"Good morning, Jean." Apparently that was the predetermined signal, because all three clambered up onto the bed to wriggle between Dana and Brady. Dana rolled over and smiled. Brady felt his heart jerk. She was beautiful. Still half-asleep, she looked more relaxed than she had in days. It was as if these children fulfilled her in ways that she hadn't expected.

"We're hungry. What are we going to have for our first breakfast as a family?" Karen asked.

"Cereal?" Brady teased.

Karen made a face. "This is special. We should have something good."

"I have canned spaghetti," Dana suggested.

Karen nixed that, too. "Uncle Brady, maybe you can make us those waffles again."

"Maybe I can." He just wanted to lie in Dana's bed for a minute longer. They couldn't have been asleep for more than forty minutes. What Dana lacked in experience, she made up for in eagerness.

Karen yanked his arm out from under the covers.

He turned his head. "You mean now?"

She nodded.

"How about an hour from now?"

"No." Ollie poked him in the arm. "Now, right now."

Dana laughed. "I guess this is a perk of not being able to make waffles." Brady could feel her hand reaching under the covers, skimming against his bare thigh, and he realized that he was naked. He grabbed the covers and held tight because Ollie, Jean and Karen were making a game of trying to pull them off.

"Dana, you don't want to see some shocked little girls," he murmured. "Help me."

Dana's laughter was hearty as she slid out of

bed. When did she have time to put on a T-shirt and panties? She pulled on a robe and called to the girls, "Let's go watch some cartoons. Uncle Brady needs a little time to get himself together. He didn't get much sleep."

"He didn't?" Ollie frowned. "We slept a long time. What was he doing?"

"Prob'ly watching television. That's what grown-ups do," Karen said importantly as she followed Dana out.

IN THE DAYS THAT FOLLOWED, Dana was surprised by how easily the family fell into a routine. The girls turned out to be extremely resilient, readily following the boundaries that she and Brady set for them, even though they'd never had any before. They'd made the decision to have Beverly cremated, and together they'd scattered her ashes into the ocean. In a rare moment of honesty, Bev had once told Brady that she was always happiest when she was in the water.

The investigators had discovered that Beverly was more than a hundred thousand dollars in debt. When she sold the house in Hollister, she'd made enough money to purchase the house they'd lived in outright. But then she'd proceeded to put more and more on her credit cards. Records on her computer showed that—toward the end—she'd made some pretty desperate wagers to get the money to pay them off.

The house had been repossessed to pay off her debt, leaving the girls with nothing. But that didn't matter, because they were still together.

Dana came to love being a wife and a parent, and those roles made her reevaluate her job. To ease her workload, she relaxed her rigid standards and allowed the students to initiate more of their own learning. In the process, she found the school became a place of greater fun and greater learning.

The girls refrained from calling her Aunt Dana at school, but the name seemed to catch on. The parents of her students were fully supportive of her unexpected marriage. The women even threw her a small Saturday luncheon, complete with wedding gifts. Her parents traveled from their home three hours north for a daylong visit, too, which made Brady inordinately nervous. For the two days prior to their arrival, he cleaned the house from top to bottom to make sure that it was presentable. He fussed about the menu and ironed everything—even the girls' jeans had creases. His worry was unfounded, though. Her parents loved him and the girls. They came laden with gifts, so many that Brady kept muttering, "This is too much. Too much." The girls just beamed, declaring that it felt like Christmas in October.

Before long, Halloween had passed and Dana was taking down the ghosts and goblins in the classroom and putting up the turkeys and cornucopias. Brady started back to work, switching his schedule so he didn't have to work nights. Every day, Dana felt a little more connected to her new family and the word *annulment* was never mentioned.

One night, after the girls were asleep, Dana read an essay that Karen had written in school. The words on the page made her realize that even though the girls could laugh and sing and sleep through the night, they would carry the scars of their childhood for a very long time. She looked up at Brady who was fixing the girls' lunches. "I think the girls need to visit their father," she said.

Brady didn't respond. He just continued smearing mustard on the six slices of bread. Dana got up and walked over to him, placing her hands on his shoulders. "Did you hear me?"

"I did. But I don't think that's something Carson wants." He spoke indifferently, almost as if he was talking about what to put on a sandwich.

"Have you talked to him about it?"

"No."

"Brady, in honor of Thanksgiving I asked the kids to write an essay about families. And I just read Karen's."

"So?"

"So it isn't hard to see that even though she considers us family, she still has issues about her real mother and father. I think she has to face them. Bev's gone. That leaves Carson. When was the last time he saw his family?"

"I think Bev took them to see him."

"You think or you know? Brady, why don't you talk about your brother?"

"There's nothing to talk about." Brady put the baloney on the bread, plopped on the tops, then efficiently wrapped them in plastic.

"I think there's a lot to talk about. You never did say what upset you so much about your visit."

"Can't we just have the girls write letters to him?" Brady finally stopped fussing with the sandwiches and faced her.

"We could. But you know—he's going to get out of prison sooner or later. If he waits, if *we* wait, it's going to be very hard for the girls to have a real relationship with him. Unless you think he's the kind of person they shouldn't have a relationship with."

"No! It's not that at all."

"What is it then?"

Brady shook his head. "I don't know." He grasped her hand. "Things are going so well for all of us. You, me, the girls."

"Which is what made me think it might be a good time for them to get to know their father."

"I just think it's too soon. I don't want to do anything that would unsettle the girls."

Dana thought about what he'd said. "You don't think they'd understand that their father can't care for them, so we're going to?"

"They might be able to, but is Jean going to think that if we take her to the prison we might leave *her* there? Will Ollie trust the strange man we tell her is her father?"

Dana held up her hands. "You're right. Let's start with writing letters. If your brother wants to follow up, he can." She walked back to the couch and put a B on Karen's essay, rereading her last sentence. *Wouldn't it be nice if all moms and dads liked their kids?*

FOR A WEEK, Brady thought about his brother. Carson's words still haunted him.

I did not do anything wrong. I did not launder money. I did not embezzle from my clients. I did not fix my books. But somehow, I still went straight to jail.

Carson had always declared his innocence. Always. As did just about every person who went to jail. But what Brady never forgot was that he'd been too angry at Carson to listen. He'd turned his back on his brother, just as Carson had done to their mother. Brady closed his eyes, trying to feel again the rage that had kept him from helping his brother. It wasn't there. It was just a sore spot—like a half healed bruise.

Even though Dana hadn't mentioned reintroducing the girls to their father again, he knew the subject wasn't dead. When three letters from Carson—one to each of the girls—arrived a few days after they'd written to him, Brady felt even worse. Every moment he spent with the girls, every night Ollie and Jean placed a good-night kiss on his cheek or Karen sat next to him as he worked just because she liked to see what he was doing, Brady fell a little more in love with them. But that love brought guilt—as if he was taking away the love that really belonged to Carson. Yes, his brother had made some mistakes, but somehow the punishment of not seeing his daughters until they were almost adults seemed especially cruel.

Late Thursday night, Brady rolled over in bed to find Dana studying him.

"Hi," he said softly. "Can't sleep?"

She smiled. "You're restless. You keep bumping into me."

"Sorry." After a long pause, he added, "I've been thinking."

"About?"

"Carson."

"What about him?"

"I think we need to take the girls to see him."

Dana's surprised pleasure made his heart beat faster. "This weekend?" she asked.

He nodded.

Her brown eyes searched his face, "Is there more?"

"Maybe."

"Maybe?"

He hesitated, then confessed. "I don't think Carson's guilty."

Dana sat up. "What? What do you mean? You said he was a criminal."

Brady sat up, too, looking straight ahead, wishing there was a television in the room to stare at, so he didn't have to look into her eyes.

"I wanted to believe he was a criminal."

"Which is different than his actually being a criminal?"

Brady's tight smile was more like a grimace. "I've never told anyone that. When Carson was arrested for laundering money through his accounting firm, I was secretly glad. I thought he was getting what he deserved. He told me he was being set up by one of his employees. But I didn't believe him. I didn't want to have anything to do with him. I'd talked to the investigators, seen their evidence. And I couldn't forget what he'd done to my mother. When she was dying she kept asking for Carson. All she wanted was to see her grandchildren. That's all. If a man was capable of that, he could do anything."

"So what makes you think he's not guilty now?"

"When I went to tell him about Bev and the custody arrangement for the girls, he said it again. He said that he didn't do it."

"And you said…"

"I didn't say much of anything. I just got out of there."

"So what does this mean?"

"I don't know. I think I need to hear his side for once, and I think you were right. We need to take the girls to see him."

LONG AFTER BRADY had fallen asleep, his arm slung over her waist, Dana remained awake. She should have felt good about Brady's confession. She'd gotten what she wanted. But she wasn't happy. A knot of dread had settled inside her. She understood Brady's sense of right and wrong, admired it. What if Carson was truly not guilty? She knew Brady would do everything in his power to prove it, to free Carson. And what would that mean for them? For the girls? For her?

CARSON WAS ALREADY WAITING in the visitors' room when Brady entered. His fingers tapped on the metal table and he gave Brady a small smile. "This can't be good news," Carson said. "This is your second visit in as many months. If there's nothing I can do about it, I don't want to hear it."

Brady sat down. "Sorry to disappoint you, but I need to know a few things."

Carson was cautious. "How are the girls?"

"They're doing really well."

"Dana?"

Brady couldn't help the smile that spread across his face. "Dana is just fine. Not many women could do what she's done. You couldn't ask for a better mother than Dana."

Carson gave Brady a speculative glance. "Married life seems to be treating you well."

"Yes." Brady couldn't begin to find the words that would describe just how well married life was treating *and* changing him. "I just need to ask you a question."

"A question?" Carson arched an eyebrow. "Okay, ask."

"If you didn't do what you're here for, who did?"

Carson was silent for a long time. Finally he shook his head. "I don't know. I just know that I didn't do it. Yes, he was my client, but I had no idea he was involved in money laundering. I just thought he was very successful at what he did. I only made the deposits, kept his books. Maybe I *should* have known, but I wasn't exactly focusing well those days—what with Mom and the problems with Bev and all."

Brady inhaled deeply. He pushed away his reaction to Carson's mention of their mother. He wasn't here to discuss that. "Could Bev have done it?" Brady asked.

Carson stared at his hands. "I've thought about it. I've thought about it every day. I didn't want to believe it. I wanted to just think that it was all a mistake."

"Did Bev have access?"

"Yes. She had access to everything. The office, the safe, the computers. She often went to dinner with the clients when I was too busy. It would have been very easy for her to—"

"But you didn't say anything."

"You and I weren't exactly on speaking terms then, if you recall."

Brady acknowledged Carson's point. "But still—"

"I was thinking about the girls and the lousy marriage and I felt it was all my fault. If I made more money, if I were a different kind of guy, if I were more like *you,* none of this would have happened. You never liked her."

Brady corrected him. "I never liked what she did to you. You changed. Mom missed you especially."

Carson swallowed. "I know I didn't make the best decisions. It was so hard. You had your choice of women, though you didn't seem interested in any of them. You were too busy working. I was very interested and no woman ever looked at me that way, until Bev."

"But you married her the next day."

"And you can talk?" Carson asked. "You

knew Dana—what?—three hours? You took the chance that you'd make it.''

Brady shook his head. ''I never thought of this marriage as lasting. It was simply so I could get custody of the girls.''

''And now?''

''Now, it's different. It's better than I thought it would be.''

Carson gave him a thin smile. ''You have what I'd hoped for. I guess you have better judgment than I do. So why all this now?''

''I'm just wondering if you can think of anything that might get you a new trial, something that I can investigate, something I didn't do before.'' Those words stuck in his throat.

Carson didn't say anything for a long time. When Brady looked over to him, he saw that his brother had started to cry.

''Thank you,'' he whispered to Brady. ''I do have some things that I've been thinking about. Five years is a long time to do nothing. I am so sorry about Mom. I wanted to bring the girls, but Bev wouldn't let them out of her sight.''

''Then you should have come by yourself.''

''I know I should have. But I didn't, and I was too late. I never got a chance to tell her that despite the way things looked, they were going to get better." He sat up and met Brady's eyes dead on. "I don't blame you for not helping then. I wouldn't have helped me, either. I'm just grateful that you've taken on the girls."

"Why wouldn't I? They're family." Brady clenched his hands. "I had no idea that Bev would mistreat them, neglect them so badly. If I had, I would have checked on them. But after you got the divorce, she told me to stay away. And I did. She wasn't pleasant."

Carson nodded, a bitter expression on his face. "She promised she'd bring the kids by once a week. She did...for a month, then it was twice a month, then twice a year. The visits stopped altogether when Ollie was about two. I didn't even know where they were after they moved."

"They ended up just on the other side of the mountain," Brady said.

"Did they ever figure out what happened to her?"

"Suicide. She had a lot of debts. I think the stress got to her. There's no other explanation."

"How are the girls adjusting?"

"Very well. Karen's the most depressed, but she gets better every day." Brady paused. "The girls sure like getting your letters."

"Thank Dana for me, because I sure do like

getting theirs.'' Carson smiled, a real smile. ''I read them over and over.''

''I will.'' The frank honesty of their conversation had Brady admitting, ''I feel like I've taken your family. I know Dana isn't Bev, but the girls are what makes our family a family.''

Carson's face didn't mask the pain he felt, and Brady once again found himself looking at the brother he'd thought he'd lost when Carson and Bev married.

''Well, given my situation, that's a good thing, right?'' Carson leaned back from the table with a smile. ''The girls have a good home. I can't ask for more than that.''

''I brought pictures.'' Brady reached into his jacket pocket and pulled out a small stack of photos.

Carson snatched them out of his hand.

Brady would have moved his chair closer to Carson, but it was bolted to the floor. He leaned over awkwardly and pointed to the smiling face in Carson's hands. ''There's Ollie. We laughed when we realized the pumpkin was almost bigger than she was.''

Brady continued, ''That's the girls in their Halloween costumes. There wasn't any place for them to go trick-or-treating, so we had a Halloween party at the school. All the students came.''

Brady watched Carson study every angle of the girls' faces. He traced their smiles with his finger, memorizing them.

''That's Karen and Jean rehearsing their parts in the Thanksgiving play. And that's Jean bobbing for apples.''

He studied the picture, his eyes riveted on Jean's laughing face. ''She's six, now, isn't she?''

''Yes.''

He picked up one of Karen. Carson's eyes began to redden as he looked at his eldest daughter, her gray eyes big and serious. ''Look at her. She looks just like Mom.''

Brady cleared his throat and got up abruptly. ''I've got to get a drink of water. You want something?''

Carson shook his head, his eyes never leaving the photos, and Brady knocked on the door for the guard.

''Are you coming back?'' Carson asked.

Brady nodded. ''Yeah. I just got something stuck in my throat.''

Brady waited outside the room for about ten minutes to give Carson time alone, then he signaled to the guard, who let him back in.

Carson put the pictures down and swallowed. "Thanks." He handed the stack back to Brady.

Brady didn't take them. "Those are for you, if you want them."

Carson put them in his pocket.

Brady swallowed. "So I have another surprise for you."

Carson gave him a wry smile, looking a lot more like the older brother that Brady knew. "Any more surprises from you and I'll probably have a heart attack."

"You might want to sit down for this."

"I am sitting."

"Oh." Brady laughed nervously. "I'd better sit down."

"Just spit it out."

"They're here."

"Who's here?"

"The girls. They're outside in the visiting area with Dana. They're waiting to meet you."

CHAPTER ELEVEN

DANA SAT on a bench in the prison's visiting area. It wasn't what she'd expected. Yes, there was the barbed wire and guards everywhere. They'd all been thoroughly searched, but the outside area actually resembled a garden. Nothing at all the way she'd imagined.

Now that they were here, she was extremely nervous. Karen sat next to her, dressed in the same dress she'd worn for the wedding. It was a beautiful fall day, the weather crisp and cool. Some of the orange and red leaves had been caught by the slight breeze, and Ollie and Jean chased them close by. They ran back and forth, determined to find the prettiest leaf.

"What's taking Uncle Brady so long?" Karen asked. "We've been out here for hours."

It wasn't much of an exaggeration. It was an hour and a half since Brady had disappeared down a hall with a prison guard.

"He's talking to your dad. Your dad didn't know we were all coming today."

"He probably doesn't want to see us."

"I don't think that's true. He answered your letters. And he said how much he missed you."

"It's easier to say stuff in a letter than face-to-face. He'll be different."

"Since he and your Uncle Brady are brothers, I would expect them to be similar. You like Uncle Brady, don't you?"

"I *love* Uncle Brady."

Dana smiled. "Then you're going to love your dad."

"Does he know about Mom?"

Dana nodded. "Uncle Brady told him."

Karen put her hand into Dana's. "Good. I wish he would come."

"There's Uncle Brady!" Ollie cried.

Dana and Karen stood up and watched him walk down the trimmed concrete path, alone.

"My dad's not with him," Karen said, disappointment crossing her face. She turned away from Brady. "See?"

"I'm sorry, Karen." Dana patted the girl on the back. "He might not have been ready today. But that's okay. We'll come back next weekend and maybe he'll change his mind. We'll keep writing letters, too."

When Brady reached them, Dana put her hand out. "You don't have to say anything. It was worth a try."

Brady shook his head and gave her a huge grin. "He went back to his cell to change into civilian clothes. The perks of minimum security on visiting day."

Dana looked around, and sure enough, the other inmates were dressed in jeans and casual cotton shirts. She hadn't even noticed. "S-so, he's going to meet them?"

Brady nodded. "He told me there's a picnic table underneath a scrub oak on the other side of this area. We're to meet him there in fifteen minutes."

Karen's eyes were wide. "My dad wants to see us?"

Brady tugged on her hair. "Yes. You'll probably be the only one who remembers him."

She wrinkled her forehead. "I'm not sure I remember him too well."

"I think you will, when you see him."

Brady and Dana sat on the bench while they waited.

"It's got to be fifteen minutes now," Ollie insisted, leaning up against Dana's knee.

"No," Dana said as she glanced at her watch. "It's only been eight minutes."

"Maybe we can start walking over now," Karen said.

"Let's give him the full fifteen minutes," Brady suggested. "You've waited five years for this."

"I think I cried when he went away." Karen swung her legs back and forth. "I didn't know where he was going." She looked around. "This isn't bad. It's not like it is on television."

Jean crawled onto Brady's lap, her hand filled with the brightly colored leaves she'd collected. "For Daddy," she told him solemnly.

"He's going to like them."

"*Now,* it's got to be time," Ollie said.

Brady checked. "Just a few more minutes." He knew that Carson wanted to be at the picnic table when the girls got there. He waited another five minutes and then stood up. "Okay, let's start walking over."

"Did you give him the pictures?" Dana asked.

Brady nodded. "He said to thank you."

"Maybe I should wait here." Dana hung back.

"No," Karen protested, grabbing Dana's hand. "You have to come, too."

"What do you think?" Dana asked Brady. "I think this is a family moment, and you should have some privacy."

Brady smiled at the woman who'd opened her heart to all of them. "You *are* the family." He wrapped his arm around Dana's waist and led her and the girls across the visiting area. It took a minute for them to find the scrub oak.

Dana was smiling in approval. "What a nice place!"

Still some distance away Brady could see Carson pacing, then when he caught a glimpse of them, he stopped and stood still. Karen slowed down and clung to Dana's hand. "There he is," she breathed.

"Why don't you go meet him?" Brady suggested. "We'll be right behind you."

Karen looked up uncertainly.

"Go on," Dana encouraged. "Go see him."

Reluctantly, Karen let go of Dana's hand and started to walk toward Carson. Brady and Dana slowed down, holding back the other two girls.

"We want to go, too," Ollie said with a whine.

"I know," Brady said. "But let Karen go first."

The closer she got to Carson the faster Karen went, until she broke into a full run and threw herself into Carson's arms. Carson wrapped his arms around Karen and lifted her off the ground, spinning her around. Brady looked down at Dana, who was searching in her purse for something. When she sniffed, he knew it was tissue.

"You are such a mush pot," he murmured teasingly, then was punished when he cleared his own throat.

They let the other little girls go, and following Karen's lead, Ollie and Jean ran full speed until Carson had all three girls in his arms.

By the time Brady and Dana got there, Ollie was sitting comfortably in Carson's lap and Jean was giving him her leaves. Karen sat beside him with one arm through his. Carson stood and gently placed Ollie on the bench. Then he walked over to the adults.

Brady was surprised when Carson went straight to Dana and pulled her into a tremendous hug.

"I don't need any introduction to you," Carson said. "Thank you for taking care of my daughters."

"You're welcome. It's been my pleasure."

"And thank you for taking this guy on."

"That's been my pleasure, too." Dana sent him a sly glance, and Brady felt his face flush.

"Dana and I thought we'd go get a bite to eat. Will the four of you be okay for an hour?"

Carson nodded. "If the girls don't mind."

Karen came up to clutch her father's hand and the younger two were all eager smiles.

"It doesn't look like they mind."

"Brady, can I talk to you a minute?" Carson asked. He extricated himself from Karen's grip and said, "I'll be right back."

Once they'd stepped away, Brady asked, "What can I do for you?"

Carson took a large manila envelope off the seat on the far side of the bench.

"What's this?" Brady took the envelope.

"I told you I've been thinking about this for the past five years, but I've been doing more than that. Maybe you can find something in there that will, uh, help."

"Any particular direction you think I should go in?"

"I trust you to go anywhere. I didn't do it." Carson started to head toward the girls. He didn't take two steps before he turned back to give Brady a bear hug. "I can't thank you enough. For everything."

As Brady and Dana walked out of the prison to find someplace to eat, Dana asked, "What did Carson give you?"

Brady shrugged. "Some papers."

"Important papers?"

"Maybe." He smiled at her and touched her cheek. "You're marvelous."

She smiled and looked at her watch. She gave him a devilish grin. "We have a whole hour without the girls."

"Aren't you hungry?"

"We have a whole hour without the girls," she repeated.

"And?"

"I've never necked in the back seat of a car. I've never made windows steamy."

"It's not as comfortable as you might think."

She raised an eyebrow and reached out a hand to touch him. "I'm not thinking about comfort. Don't you know any good places to park?"

Fortunately, Brady did.

BRADY STARED at the documents in front of him. If it was possible to feel both head-rushing excitement and true regret at the same time, then that was what he was experiencing. There was definitely evidence that Carson was innocent.

He glanced at the clock. Dana would be back with the girls in a little over an hour. He didn't know how he was going to tell her. His brother's lawyer had been so incompetent that he'd allowed Carson to take a plea rather than go to court. Brady felt awful. He should have helped his brother find a lawyer. Even the guilty deserved decent representation.

Brady got up and fixed dinner absently. Dana and the girls arrived home, but he remained distracted.

"Are you okay?" Dana asked from across the table where she was helping Jean cut her pork chop into little pieces.

"Yes," he said.

"You're pretty quiet."

"I have good news about Carson."

Dana smiled with genuine pleasure. "Really! That's wonderful! What happened?"

He tilted his head toward Karen and said, "There's still a few things to look into, before I can talk about it."

Dana understood the reason for his vagueness and didn't ask anything more.

"Is this about us?" Karen asked, her voice concerned.

"No, honey," he lied. "Finish your potatoes. Do you have a lot of homework?"

"No. I finished it in class today."

Brady looked to Dana for confirmation. "I'm afraid she did. Maybe I should give her more."

"Not fair," protested Karen. "I want to watch a show on the Disney Channel."

"Well, I think that can be arranged," Dana said.

"It goes until ten," Karen put in slyly.

"You know the rule. You can watch until nine and then we'll tape the rest so you can see it tomorrow."

Karen pushed her bottom lip out. "It's not the same as watching it all the way through."

"We could tape the whole thing, then, watch it tomorrow. That way tonight you can start on the report that's due next week," Dana reminded her.

Karen jumped up with her empty plate. "That's okay. I'll set the VCR to tape after nine."

DANA WATCHED BRADY from the kitchen table where she was working on her lesson plans. He chuckled at Ollie's knock-knock jokes, but his mind wasn't there. After dinner, he'd gone right back to the card table he'd set up in the corner just for the documents he needed to work on

Carson's case. She'd been disconcerted by his news. What did good news for Carson mean for her?

Finally, at nine o'clock Karen popped the tape in and after one more plea to stay up, she went to bed, joining her sisters who'd been there for an hour. After Dana had tucked her in, she went into the living room to find Brady sitting on the couch. His face was pensive, and Dana felt her heart thud under her ribs.

"Hi," she said as she moved to sit next to him.

He looked up at her, a small smile on his face. "We need to talk."

She studied the lines on the face that had become so dear to her. "That doesn't sound so good."

"Dana, it's not really bad news, depending on how you look at it."

"That sounds even worse," she observed. Then she took a deep breath. "Okay, hit me with it."

"It's about Carson."

Dana sat straighter, feeling his eyes search her face. She nodded and reached for his hand, surprised at how cold it was. She asked, "Does this have anything to do with that?" She gestured toward the card table.

He sighed. "Everything."

Dana thought her heart would jump out of her chest.

BRADY STARED at the wall where the girls had hung their latest artwork. Then he gathered his courage and looked Dana right in the eye. She was afraid, and he didn't blame her. What he had to say was going to hurt her.

"Just tell me, Brady. Just tell me."

"He didn't do it."

"Didn't do what?"

"He didn't do what he was convicted of."

"But I thought you said the evidence was there."

"I know. But he has documentation that proves otherwise. It was all Bev. She wanted more money than Carson was making, so she found another way to make it. To cover herself, she forged Carson's signature. If his lawyer had even bothered to read the documents, he would have realized that what was in the computer didn't match what was in Carson's books."

Dana sat very still. "And?"

"And when I started to dig into one thing, other things began popping up."

"Like what?" Her voice was very low.

"Like Bev had enough money while Carson

was working. Money she didn't get from him. And once he was arrested, the money dried up. She must have been the one doing the laundering. Without a legitimate business to use as a front, she wasn't any use to them."

"So that explains the debt."

Brady nodded. "If you go back over her credit record, you'll see how she continued living at the same standard until she had to sell the house. I'm sure the girls were being neglected before that, but after moving, Bev must have gone completely downhill. She'd spend more and have less and less for food."

There was a long silence. "So what does this mean?" Dana asked eventually.

"It means that Carson didn't do it."

Dana furrowed her forehead, her breathing rapid. "But if he had all this evidence, why didn't he just turn it over instead of going to prison?"

Brady was silent. "Dana. He did that. But because he had an inexperienced public defender who preferred to plea rather than expose his inadequacies in court, this stuff was ignored."

"But shouldn't Carson have known what to do?"

"He was an accountant, and he thought he'd done what he could by giving this information to his lawyer. But that wasn't all. He asked me for help. I didn't give it to him." Guilt tore at him. The whole situation was his fault. He turned to Dana praying that she would know what he was trying to do. "So I need you to understand that's why I'm going to pursue this."

"How? What are you saying?"

"I'm going to see if I can get Carson exonerated. There's enough evidence—"

"To free him?" Dana's eyes went wide.

"I can't say for sure, but I think so. I think it will get him out pretty quickly."

"Quickly. As in a year?"

Brady shook his head. "As in weeks."

"Weeks?" Her voice raised an octave.

"Believe it or not, the state frowns upon incarcerating innocent men." Brady was serious. "If I present this to the right people, they would make it a priority, especially since this also implicates a lot of other people they've been trying to catch."

DANA SAT BACK and put her hands into her lap, the consequences of what Brady was saying washing through her like freezing water.

"Well," she managed to say. "That's good

news, isn't it?'' She didn't know why she was ready to cry.

Brady shifted closer to her. ''Yes, it is good news, but—''

''We'll still have custody, right?'' Dana said with desperate hope, even though she thought she knew the answer. ''At least until Carson can find a job. He's going to be returning to a different world from the one he left. He went in a family man. Now he won't have the family.''

''He does have a family,'' Brady said gently.

Dana shook her head in denial. ''No. *We* have the family. Remember, we're their family.''

''Carson doesn't deserve to be in prison and he doesn't deserve not to have custody of his children.''

Dana's head was spinning. She couldn't believe that this was happening again. She'd given her heart to children whose parents wouldn't, and now those kids were going to be taken away. And *Brady* was going to be the one who did it.

''You didn't think he was innocent five years ago.'' She leaped to her feet, releasing Brady's hand. Just as quickly, he reached out and put his hand on her forearm.

''Don't do this,'' Brady pleaded as he pulled her back to the sofa.

"Don't do what? Don't care? Don't think about what's going to happen to those girls when their father gets out of prison? You see Karen every day. She's just beginning to really settle in here. She's finally learning how to be a kid. And you want to turn things upside down again."

He nodded in sympathy. "It's going to be hard. They *are* just getting settled in with us. But they are Carson's kids, and he deserves the chance to look after them…to love them."

"If he'd loved them, he would have tried to keep in touch."

"He's been in prison, Dana." Brady's words were sharp. "He couldn't chase after Bev when she moved. He couldn't demand that Bev bring the girls to see him. Please, Dana." He pulled her into his arms, but Dana didn't want to be held by him. She knew what he was saying was right, but her pain and anger superseded that. She hadn't wanted to care for these girls, hadn't wanted to love them. But Brady had insisted and now he was planning to snatch them away again.

"You knew this wasn't permanent. You knew *that*."

"Three months ago, I knew that," she said. "And I knew then that our marriage would end when our custody arrangement did. So I guess you're telling me it's over, too.''

BRADY FELT THE BLOOD DRAIN from his face. He'd known she wasn't going to take losing the girls well, but after everything they'd gone through, he hadn't thought she still believed the girls were the only reason they were married. ''Why would I say that?'' He was surprised by how stiff his voice sounded.

''Wasn't that the bargain? When I wasn't needed anymore, we'd get an annulment? Isn't that what you promised?''

''I didn't promise anything like that,'' Brady denied. ''I didn't know what to expect. You know how hard that time was.''

''So when the girls go back to their father, then we're done. Right?''

Brady felt his world begin to fall apart. He didn't want the marriage to end, but he didn't want Dana to stay in a relationship when she believed he'd betrayed her.

''Is that what you want?''

She was silent for a long time.

''Dana?'' he prompted.

She shrugged and wouldn't look at him.

''Dana, you need to talk to me.''

When she finally turned, her eyes were red. "My mind says that I shouldn't. That you are the most incredible man who has ever graced my life. But my heart says that if you can take away these girls, then you can take away anything."

He didn't understand how she could think he was doing this because he wanted to hurt her. "I'm not taking the girls from you. They were never yours."

"Don't say that. They *were* mine." Her voice held a note of true hysteria. "They were *my* three girls. *You* gave them to me. Don't you remember?" Brady wanted to hug her, but she shoved his hands away. "Don't you remember I told you I couldn't take the girls? I did that once before and this time is worse because—"

"Because why?" He cocked his head at her.

"Forget I said that."

"Say it—" Brady demanded

"No."

"Because you and I fell in love? Because you finally had a real family?" He raised his hands in the air. "Well, gee. Next time I become responsible for three abandoned girls and persuade a beautiful, caring woman to help me with them, I'll make sure I don't fall in love with her." Brady stretched out his hands to her. "Don't you see,

Dana? Don't you see how ridiculous you're being? It's not like the children will go very far. I can find Carson a place around here. The girls could even continue to attend your school. We'd see them all the time. We were given a gift. We were given the gift of love. And now you're throwing it away.''

''No.'' Dana took a deep breath. ''I'm not throwing it away. You did that.''

DANA COULDN'T TALK to Brady anymore. The hurt in his eyes was more than she could bear. ''I'm going to bed. We can discuss it later.''

''No,'' Brady said. ''You can't run away from this. Closing yourself off won't lessen the pain. Love and loss are part of the same thing, but that doesn't mean you shouldn't love. Do you think it won't hurt me to see those girls go? It's going to hurt like hell. But Dana, I know that Carson is a good father. I know that those girls belong to him.''

Dana shook her head, the tears spilling over. ''*No!* They belong to us. *We* have custody. You're just doing this because you think you have to.''

Brady looked sad. ''That's where you're wrong, Dana. They are Carson's daughters. But if you want, you can still have me.''

Dana couldn't look at him. She said distantly, "I'd prefer if you slept out here tonight."

"Dana, don't do this to us."

"You do realize that you're the one who has to tell the girls that they're going to live with a stranger. I won't."

"Dana, that's not fair to Carson. We were strangers and they've thrived under our care. Carson's their father. You have to believe this is the right thing. This isn't going to finish for them the way it did for Adam. Carson isn't going to go off the deep end. He has three precious beings to live for. The same ones who helped us."

"Helped us do what?"

"Helped us learn how to live."

Dana shook her head. "All this has done is remind me why I didn't want to get involved. You know, I'm sorry I ever met you."

Brady shuttered his expression, and she knew she'd finally gone too far. "Fine," he said. "When this is over, it will be like you never met me."

CHAPTER TWELVE

TIME SEEMED TO BE against Dana. By Thanksgiving, Brady informed her that there'd been a special hearing and Carson had been exonerated. He was expected to be released in two short weeks. Rather than perpetrate a farce, Dana stiffly requested that she, alone, take the girls to her parents for Thanksgiving. She pretended not to see the hurt on Brady's face when he agreed to stay behind. Usually a favorite holiday, the whole day was miserable. She felt terrible when she'd had to answer her parents' questions about Brady. She didn't want to say he was at home eating a frozen dinner, so she said he was working. Fortunately, only Karen seemed to realize something wasn't right.

After that day, Brady kept his distance from her, which made it easy for Dana to justify her behavior. It proved that the reason for their marriage had been the girls alone. She hadn't been wrong, she told herself. However, when it came time to tell the girls they would be going back to their father, Dana sat right next to him, a tight smile glued to her face.

"What are you saying?" Karen asked, her eyes swiveling back and forth between the two adults.

"The authorities came to realize your dad was innocent all along, so he's being released."

"Released?"

"What does that mean?" Ollie asked impatiently.

"It means that he's going to get out of prison." Karen's eyes glowed. "That's great. We can see him whenever we want. Or maybe he can move in here."

Dana looked at Brady, who cleared his throat.

"No, Karen," Brady started.

"No?" Her voice became very suspicious. "Where is he going to live?"

"We found him a nice house not far from where you used to live. It's got four bedrooms."

Karen furrowed her forehead. "Why would he need a place so big?"

Dana inhaled deeply and spoke for the first time. "He wants each of you to have your own room."

"For when we visit?" Karen asked. Her voice was hopeful, but her gray eyes were worried.

"No, for when you go live with him," Dana said softly.

There were three seconds of silence before the whole room felt like an eruption had taken place.

"You're getting rid of us!" Karen accused.

"No, no. It's not like that at all. He's your father, honey," Dana tried to explain, but her voice was drowned out by the sound of blood rushing in her ears.

"I have a father. Uncle Brady." She turned to him. "You're my father now. Remember, you got custody. Remember? We don't belong to my father. We belong to you and Aunt Dana."

Almost the exact words that Dana had said to Brady, but he didn't look as if he'd relent now any more than he had then.

"I know it's going to be hard."

"What are they saying, Karen?" Ollie asked, tugging on her sister's shirt, ready to cry.

"They're saying that they want to get rid of us and give us to our father."

Jean and Ollie began to cry, and Dana did what she could to comfort them. She couldn't look at Brady. She just knew that she would never be able to forgive him.

Later, after she'd dried the girls' tears and tucked them into bed, Brady stopped her in the hall. "You may not agree, Dana, but doing this now *is* easier than it would be next year."

He might have been right, but she didn't want to believe him. She couldn't imagine much worse than this.

TO HELP THE TENSION that bristled every time he and Dana were in the same room, Brady switched to the night shift so she didn't have to ignore him while he was there. He found an apartment for himself and spent his free time at Carson's new house, working with a contractor to remodel it to Carson's specs.

He stopped by Dana's, no longer home to him, to fix dinner and the girls' lunches for the next day before he started his shift. Dana at best was polite. In one of the few conversations they had, Dana had tried to plead for the girls to have Christmas with them, but Brady was determined to reunite the girls with their father in time for Christmas.

"He's missed five Christmases, Dana," was all he'd said.

"I've never even had one" was her stomach-twisting retort.

Soon the girls began the agonizing task of trying to pack up their possessions. They'd come to that little house with almost nothing. Now there were shelves of books, a slew of stuffed animals and a closet full of clothes.

Brady had already moved most of his stuff by that point. "No use taking up all your space" was how he'd explained it to Dana. The girls realized his things were gone and clung to him when he was around. As for his wife, she accepted the changes he made without comment or emotion, and he couldn't help but wish for their old relationship back. He knew there was more to their relationship than the girls. But she didn't, and she wouldn't let him close enough to let him prove it.

ON THE DAY they were to take the girls to their new house, Dana woke at 3:00 a.m. with a feeling of dread. The girls weren't going to end up like Adam. She knew Carson was going to be a good father. Ever since they'd found out he was innocent, she'd taken the girls to visit him every weekend. Carson had drilled her relentlessly about Karen, Jean and Ollie, and she had come to genuinely like him. He was a gentler version of his brother. He noticed small things, like Jean's small ring and Karen's dolphins. But that didn't make Dana feel any better. She stared at the dark ceiling and wondered how she'd live without those girls and couldn't even begin to think about how she would manage to survive after they'd left.

After today.

Today was the day Dana was supposed to give them to their father. That Dana would see them daily at school was small consolation. She would teach them, but that was all.

She felt someone staring at her and rolled over on her side.

"Aunt Dana?"

She smiled in the direction of the small voice. "Karen. You're supposed to be sleeping."

Karen took that as an invitation to join her in the bed. "I can't sleep. I'm really scared." Dana felt Karen's bony elbow dig into her ribs. She shifted to put her arm around Karen's shoulders.

"What are you scared about?"

"I don't want to live with my dad."

Dana didn't want her living with her dad, either, but she needed to be the adult. "It's going to take some adjustment from both of you. But you're going to be fine. It's all going to work out." And Dana didn't doubt it. Karen was going to have her happily-ever-after.

"What if he doesn't like us when he lives with us?" Her voice was uncertain, small. Dana took a deep breath and squeezed her eyes shut. Finally,

Karen was learning what it was like to trust an adult.

"He can't help but love you."

"How do you know that for sure?"

"Because I had thought I'd never love anyone, but as soon as I started living with you, I loved you," Dana whispered, tightening her arm around Karen.

"Then why do you want to get rid of us?"

"I don't want to get rid of you, but you belong with your father, not with me."

"What if we don't like him? Can we come back and live with you and Uncle Brady?"

Dana was silent. Of course the girls realized there was tension between her and Brady, but obviously they thought it would work out.

"You're going to love your dad. He's missed too much of your lives and he wants to make up for it."

"But I'm going to miss you and Uncle Brady."

Dana felt a tear slide down her temple. "I'm going to miss you, too."

"Is Uncle Brady going to miss us?"

Another tear followed the path of the first. "Yes. He's going to miss you very much."

"So you two get to be together and we have to

go away." Karen clearly didn't think the arrangement was fair. "Do you love him more than us?"

Dana was silent as she tried to find an answer for Karen. Finally, she said slowly, "I don't love Uncle Brady more than you. I love your Uncle Brady differently. I think I started to love him *because* of you. Then somewhere I just started loving him for him." She realized that her words were true. She did love Brady. She loved the man he was, the man he *had* to be—even though he knew he would hurt her if he did the right thing.

"I don't think you should be mad at him because he got my dad out of jail."

"I'm not mad at him about that. Your dad should have never gone to jail in the first place."

"I heard you arguing."

Dana stroked Karen's hair. "You weren't supposed to hear us."

"You said you were sorry that you ever met him. Are you sorry you ever met us?"

Dana fought to speak over her heart, now lodged in her throat. "No. I'm very glad I met you. I was wrong to say what I said to your Uncle Brady. Sometimes when we hurt, we say things we don't mean."

"Do you wish we could stay with you forever and ever?"

What a question! Dana didn't answer for a long time. "I would wish it if you didn't have a daddy who loved you as much as your daddy does."

"Do you love me?"

Dana couldn't say the words. Adam had asked her to as they sat together waiting at the park.

"Say that you love me," Adam begged. "Say that you'll always, always, always love me."

Dana just hugged him close. "I do love you. I'll always, always, always love you."

"When I'm grown up, can we get married?"

Dana had to laugh. "When you're grown up, I'll be an old, old lady. And there will be lots of young, pretty girls who will be standing in line to marry you."

"I'll want you, because you love me."

It had taken every ounce of strength that Dana had had to force a smile on to her face so that when he went back to his mother, he would believe it was for the best. She tugged Karen even closer.

"Yes. I love you and I love Jean and I love Ollie."

"And Uncle Brady? You love Uncle Brady, don't you?"

"Yes. Uncle Brady, too." There—she'd admitted it.

"What do you love best about me?" Karen asked.

"I love your smile, your nose, the way you help your sisters. I love that you make me smile."

"So what happens when I'm gone? Who's going to make you smile?"

Later, when Dana put Karen back into her bed to get at least a few hours of sleep, she sat in the room and watched Ollie curl up close to Jean. Who was going to make her smile? What was going to fill the hole that these three girls would leave behind?

By the time Brady arrived to pick up the girls, Dana's eyes felt as if they were made of lead, partly from the lack of sleep, partly from the weight of sadness.

"Everyone ready?" Brady asked, his voice overly cheerful.

"I can't find my shoes," Ollie hollered. She had only one sock on. "I don't want to go."

"Ollie." Brady knelt in front of her. "We've talked about this. You're going to live with your dad."

"*You're* my dad."

"No, he's not, stupid," Karen snapped uncharacteristically. "He's our uncle. Our dad just got out of jail."

"Your dad loves you," Brady told Ollie, and then addressed Karen. "Your dad is being pardoned. Do you know what pardoned means?"

"Yes. It's something that says you didn't do what you were put in jail for." Karen rattled off the explanation with a preadolescent roll of her eyes.

"Exactly. A pardon says that the government made a mistake and is sorry he ever had to go there."

Ollie's eyes filled with tears. "Why can't we be a family?"

Dana watched as Brady glanced up at her. She didn't see regret or any other emotion on his face. "Because you have your own family to make."

"Who's going to take care of Aunt Dana?" Ollie struggled to put on her shoe.

Dana, her sinuses hurting from the tears she held back, sat down next to Ollie and helped her with her shoe.

"Aunt Dana has her job." His voice was so harsh that Dana bit her lip. Was that how cold he thought she was? That teaching would take the place of his hugs and kisses or his tender lovemaking?

"If he's mean to us, can we come back to live

with you and Aunt Dana?'' Ollie asked, her hands
on Dana's as she fumbled with the little buckle.

Brady walked out of the house to the car, leaving her to deal with Ollie's question. While she
did, she remembered the look he'd given her on
his way out—the one that told her she was the
last woman on the earth that he would want to
live with.

THE DRIVE TO CARSON'S HOUSE seemed to take
forever. Brady could feel the tension in the car.
Dana hadn't wanted to come, but he appreciated
that she had. It would make the move easier for
all the girls. He'd been giving her the space she'd
requested, and it wasn't boding well for their marriage. When he'd all but moved out, she didn't
even blink. Now, Dana sat, her back stiff, staring
out the window.

"It's going to be okay. They're going to be
okay,'' he said to her in an undertone.

She didn't respond, just continued to stare out
the window.

"They weren't ours in the first place,'' he tried
again.

Her head swiveled toward him. "I just don't
have the ability to meter out the quantity of my

love. And I can't stop loving them because I'm no longer their guardian.''

Brady looked into the rearview mirror, glad that Karen had on her headphones and Ollie and Jean were too engrossed in pointing out trees to listen to the conversation.

''Don't worry,'' she said, noticing the direction of his gaze. ''I haven't said anything to them.''

''I didn't think you had.''

Dana gave a bitter laugh. ''I can see it on your face.''

''You don't know what I think.''

''You *think* it's going to be all right because, after all, I have my teaching. That for some reason, teaching can take the place of living, breathing children who crawl into the bed each morning.'' Her voice was hurt and Brady cocked his head to the side.

It was the first emotion she'd shown in weeks.

''I didn't mean it like that.''

''Okay.'' She stared out the window again.

''If you want to know, I think you're a compassionate woman who's been hurt before and is being torn by doing the right thing.''

''And you? How do you feel about this?'' Dana asked, her voice so low that he could barely hear her.

"Me?" He was startled.

"Aren't you going to miss this?"

"Miss what?"

"Miss…us." She sounded wistful.

Brady was very still. He cleared his throat and asked cautiously, "Define 'us.'"

She looked at him with tears in her eyes.

"You need for me to define 'us'?"

"I just want to know if you think about us the same way I do."

"Us. You, me, the girls. That's the 'us' I'm talking about."

Brady couldn't explain how disappointed he was by that answer. If she'd been talking about just the two of them—that would be different. But for her the "us" was a package deal. A ready-made family.

"There *is* no us." The words came out sharper than he intended. All this time, he'd thought they'd been working as a team—something he believed would be the foundation for something truly permanent. Yes, the loss of the girls would leave a tremendous hole in their lives, but that didn't mean that he and Dana didn't have a relationship.

"Of course there is an us. The last months have been all five of us together."

"And when there's only two? When the girls go back to their father, will there still be an us?" He didn't want to be rude, but he had to make her realize that the "us" she imagined—her, the kids and him—could not happen. He was who he was. Not just the father doll in her little playhouse. He wasn't anything but Brady Moore. But he was willing to stay with her and make their marriage work.

"You don't understand," Dana muttered finally.

"On the contrary." He felt his heart starting to ache. "I think I understand much too well."

"Don't fight," Karen begged suddenly from the back seat.

"We're not fighting," Brady said. "Sometimes Dana and I just disagree on things."

DANA COULDN'T SAY anything to Karen. If Brady thought that whether or not there was an "us" was only a small disagreement, then she had completely misread him. Maybe he'd come to realize she really was a spinster schoolteacher and he was trying to find a way to go back to his old life. Funny, that hurt more than the thought of the girls leaving. She knew they weren't hers, that they belonged with Carson, and eventually she would come to feel good about the decision. But right now, she was devastated to think that she was going to return to her old, lonely life.

Dana hung back when they got to Carson's house. It looked a bit sterile, without the personal touches that would make it a home, but that would be Carson's job.

"Our house is green!" Karen said in delight. "Is he here?"

"I think so."

As if on cue, Carson stepped onto the porch. He was smiling, and as she did every time she saw him, Dana looked for the resemblance between the two brothers. Maybe in the way they held themselves. Maybe around the eyes. But the open delight on Carson's face was something she never saw on Brady's. It wasn't fair that the man she loved was so much more contained than his brother. The men embraced and the girls stared up at the tall man who was their father.

"Dad." Karen sounded old again.

"Karen."

"This is Ollie." Her hand gestured to her right. "And this is Jean."

Carson nodded. "I remember. We saw each other last week."

"Oh, yeah."

After a long pause, Brady opened the door. "Why don't you go in? You girls can see your rooms. Karen will get her own room and Ollie and Jean are going to share for a while. Your dad picked out bunk beds for you."

Dana's heart was in the pit of her stomach. They'd talked about getting bunk beds for the girls. Carson gave her a small smile and gestured for her to join them.

"Coming, Dana?" Brady asked.

Reluctantly, she followed them in.

She heard Karen squeal and then come running out of a bedroom.

"Ohmigosh! Aunt Dana, you *need* to see this." Karen took her hand and tugged her in the direction of a room.

Dana hadn't known what to expect, but the home looked wonderful. They walked on brand-new carpet past the simple but classic furniture, until they stood in front of a door that had a colorful "Karen" painted across it. Dana looked inside and smiled.

"It's a canopy bed," Karen cried. "And I have my own desk. And look at this bookcase! I've never had anything like this before." She ran her hands over the books on the shelf. "It's pink!"

"It certainly is pink."

A beautiful girl's room. Pink fluff, retro pastel furniture. Someone had worked very hard to get the room this way. She couldn't imagine that it was Brady.

"Your dad picked all this out for you." Brady's voice came over Dana's shoulder. She was startled to find him standing right behind her, Carson beside him.

"He did?" Karen expressed her disbelief. "How could he?"

"He found them in catalogs and ordered them for you."

Karen looked uncertain. She stared at the man standing in the doorway, his hands jammed in his pockets, his eyes shyly downcast. Dana and Brady moved farther into the room so Karen could see her father. "You did?" she asked him. "How come?"

It took a long time for Carson to answer. Finally, he said gruffly, "Because you're my little girl."

Karen stared at him without a word. Then Carson crouched so he was eye level with her. He held his arms open, but Karen backed away. Carson couldn't hide the hurt on his face.

"Do you remember me?" Karen's eyes filled with tears.

"Of course I remember you. You're my little girl."

"I'm not a little girl. I'm eleven."

"No matter how old you get, you'll always be my little girl. Always."

"Even when you were in jail?"

"Especially when I was in jail. I thought about you all the time."

"But you never remembered my birthday."

"I remembered every one of your birthdays."

Carson smiled slowly and with a cry of joy Karen launched herself into his arms. He pulled her close, squeezing hard.

Dana turned away, brushing past Brady, who held out a hand but pulled it back when she rebuffed him. Whether she liked it or not, Brady Moore was a very wise man. But she couldn't admit that yet. She needed time to heal her own hurts first. Pasting a friendly smile on her face, she peeked into Jean and Ollie's room and found a lovely castle bunk set, complete with a turret playhouse attached to the side. Jean was sitting on the top. She gave Dana a big grin and Dana crossed over to her.

"I love you," Jean whispered. "We have our own closets!"

"I love you, too." Dana looked around the

room that was for just Ollie and Jean and realized it was bigger than the room all three had shared at her house. Here, the girls would be sleeping in their own beds rather than sharing the pull-out couch.

"There's room for everyone here," Ollie declared as she opened the box filled with her stuffed animals. She pulled them out, then carried them over to her bed to arrange them carefully. "But *I* get the pillow," she told them.

Dana sat on Ollie's bed, hugging the long spotted neck of a giraffe. She bounced a couple of time. "This feels very, very good. I think you're going to like it here." Dana got off the bed and got on her hands and knees to check out the turret.

"As much as I like it at your house?" Ollie asked on her knees beside Dana. She leaned up against Dana, wriggling her head under Dana's arm.

"Yes. I think you're going to like it even more."

Carson poked his head in the door. "You're going to stay for lunch, right, Dana?"

Dana hurriedly backed out of the turret. She gave him an embarrassed smile. "Uh, sure."

Carson smiled. "Good. I was afraid you had to

get back. Brady said you might have a prior commitment.''

She shook her head. ''No, no commitments.''

''Come on. Brady is going to give us the tour of all his upgrades.''

Dana reluctantly rose to her feet. She didn't want to see what Brady had done to the house. She didn't want to witness the painstaking care he'd taken to rebuild his brother's life. However, she couldn't keep from running her hand over the woodwork in the kitchen or admiring the handsome ceiling moldings. She opened the brand-new refrigerator, pushed the automatic ice dispenser. She also noticed that whenever she got close to Brady, he moved away so that Carson or the girls were always between them.

After the tour, Dana went back and forth between the girls' rooms to help unpack their belongings.

''There's so much space,'' Karen said. ''I think I'm going to have to get Dad to buy me more clothes.''

Dana had a hard time smiling, but she did and added, ''Well, if you want to go shopping, you know where to find me.''

''We'll still be friends like that, right?'' Karen asked. ''You'll still be my aunt and everything.''

Dana was silent. This wasn't the time to tell the girls about the divorce. So she just nodded.

"Good." Karen looked relieved. "I'm glad we're still going to be family."

Karen's words hit Dana like a slap. It was such a simple concept that Dana wondered how she'd missed it. As long as she was married to Brady, they *were* family.

During lunch, Dana sat on the porch nibbling her sandwich, staring down the long dirt road. Carson came up behind her, his paper plate in his hand. "Do you mind if I sit here?"

"What?" Dana was miles away, thinking about what Karen had said. She glanced up at him and then shook her head. "No, not at all."

"I never really properly thanked you." He said, stretching his legs out.

"For what?" she asked, and took a big bite of her sandwich just to do something.

"For stepping in when the girls really needed help. I know you're responsible for bringing them to visit the first time. I don't think Brady would have ever come to visit me on his own. He'd never visited before that." Carson gave a small laugh. "Thank you for giving me back my children."

She shrugged. Despite the fact he was thin, his

face showed none of the bitterness she expected to see in a man wrongly imprisoned. He did look like Brady, but his eyes were gentler and more inviting, especially when he looked at his girls. His three girls.

They were never mine. Dana cleared her throat and confessed, "It was Brady who worked out the whole thing. He's a good man."

"You love those girls."

"Yes," she said. She glanced back at the house and knew the truth. "But they need to live with you."

"If I was still in prison, you'd have them." His eyes were probing.

She nodded. "The thought has crossed my mind." She gave him a wan smile. "But then, they wouldn't get to know their father until it was too late."

"Anyway," Carson cleared his throat. "Thank you. The girls were lucky to have someone like you love them."

Dana didn't want to ask, but the words slipped out before she could stop them. "Have you talked much to Brady lately?" She wanted to seem casual, unconcerned. She left out the "about me," but Carson picked that up.

Even so, Carson took his time answering. Finally, he said, his voice measured, "He's told me some things in confidence."

"Any advice you can give me?" She stared out at the road, feeling tears begin to form. These were tears for Brady, not the girls.

Carson nodded. "Follow your heart even if you're afraid of getting hurt."

CHAPTER THIRTEEN

As MUCH AS DANA hated to admit it, Brady had been right. Carson was able to give the children so much more than she was. During the rest of the day, he told them how he'd already been able to resume some of his accounting practice. He still had one or two clients willing to take a chance on him.

For Dana, even knowing that the girls would be fine couldn't fill the emptiness that the three were leaving behind them. She couldn't seem to forget that she was going back to her old hollow life. Whether she liked it or not, the girls and Brady had changed her. She couldn't retreat into the oblivion she'd existed in before.

This new place of wanting was unpleasant. She sighed. Feeling sorry for herself wasn't going to get her anywhere, but watching Brady keep his distance from her all day had hurt. Didn't he realize that she needed to blame *someone* for the pain. She was being unfair, she knew, but did he have to accept it and move on so quickly?

As she and Brady got in the car to go home, Karen came running over and tapped on the window.

Dana rolled down the window. "Yes," she asked.

"I forgot my notebook at your house. Can you bring it?" She looked anxious.

"Oh, don't worry about it. I'll just see you at school on Monday."

"I can call you, right?"

"Sure. You can call me anytime you want." Dana hugged her through the window. "You're going to be fine."

"I'm going to miss you." Karen's eyes filled with tears. "I love you."

"I love you, too. And the missing will just last a little bit. You'll do fine. You'll all do fine."

"Okay." Karen wasn't happy, but she took her hands off the car and backed up toward the house where her sisters were waiting to wave goodbye.

The drive home was silent and strained.

Finally, Dana said, "You did an amazing job in the house."

"Thanks." Brady stared straight ahead at the road. He was close enough for her to touch, but there was a barrier around him that she didn't have the courage to cross.

"The girls' rooms are great."

"Carson took a lot of time choosing what he wanted."

"The furniture fit perfectly."

"We measured."

"Oh."

Dana couldn't think of anything else to say. After he pulled up in front of her house, they both got out of the car. Brady started fishing around in his pocket for his keys.

"Do you want to come in?" she asked. Maybe this was when they could start over.

He hesitated and then shook his head. "No. I've got to go to work."

"Oh, okay."

"I get off at three."

"I'll be asleep." She didn't know why she said that. She didn't know why she just didn't tell him to come over whenever he got off work. That was what she really wanted.

He held out something to her.

"What's this?"

"Your house key."

She backed away from it, shaking her head.

"No, that's okay. You might need it for something."

"I wouldn't think so."

"What if you need to get in?" Her voice sounded feeble to her as she searched for reasons for him to keep the key.

"What for?" he asked, and seemed to be waiting.

Because this is where you live. But Dana couldn't make the words come out, so she reached out and took the key.

He shoved his hands in the pockets of his jeans. "So I guess this is it."

Dana nodded, too numb and too proud to fling herself into his arms and tell him she was wrong. That even if the girls had stayed, they wouldn't make up for his absence. But the only thing she could seem to say was, "I guess so."

He nodded and with quick strides got into his truck and drove away.

Dana waited until she couldn't see his taillights anymore before she started to cry.

At three o'clock Dana was sitting on the couch staring at one of Brady's nature programs. She kept the volume down low so she could hear the crunch of his tires on the gravel. But he didn't come and she fell asleep on the couch, thinking that she could smell him.

In the morning, she saw the leftovers of the last dinner they'd had together, neatly wrapped in plastic. Evidence of Brady was everywhere. The locks on her door, the vegetables in her refrigerator, the sparkle on her floors, all were Brady.

The school days weren't so bad. Her students kept her busy and she got to see Karen, Jean and Ollie. She also saw a great deal of Carson, who confided that Brady's continued financial support had made it possible for him to spend time getting to know his daughters, rather than having to go back to work full time. Brady's generosity didn't surprise her. It only made her ache for him more. The girls seemed to miss their uncle, too, though Carson was trying hard to alleviate that. To be close to them, he'd even volunteered to help around the school.

Dana accepted his offer. There were more repairs than she could handle herself. So Carson dropped the girls off, then donned a pair of coveralls and did everything from repainting the playground lines to preparing the vegetable garden for winter. He took care of their gopher problem and supervised the students at recess and lunch. More often than not, he and the girls stayed for dinner.

Carson was as adept in the kitchen as Brady, with an even wider repertoire.

Dana sniffed in appreciation when she walked into the house. The aroma of baked chicken filled the room. December was proving to be bitterly cold and the sizzling of vegetables, and Ollie and Jean laughing, warmed the house more than her furnace would. Her cheeks still stinging, she closed her eyes, wishing it was Brady in the kitchen cooking.

"That smells great," she said.

"My specialty," Carson said with a grin. "I hope you don't mind."

"Oh, I always mind men coming in my house and cooking dinner."

"Karen said she needed to use your encyclopedia for her report."

"Don't you have that online?" Dana asked the girl who sprawled on the floor in front of the television. Karen grinned back at her.

"I like studying here. Our house is too big." She shot a look at her father. "Sorry, Dad, but it is. It's cozy here. The only person missing is Uncle Brady." She gasped and covered her mouth.

"That's okay," Dana dismissed. "You're right. It's just not the same without him."

"He asks about you all the time," Karen assured her.

"He does?" Dana was ashamed about how desperate she was to hear that. "How is he?"

"He's good. He comes over a lot." Karen returned to her homework after Carson gave her a warning by clearing his throat.

She walked over to Carson. "Is that true?"

"Is what true?" he asked, suddenly very absorbed in his veggies.

"Is it true that Brady goes over to your place a lot?"

Carson nodded.

"You live five miles from here." She couldn't help feeling hurt.

"If that," Carson agreed.

"But he never stops by."

"Maybe he thinks you don't want to see him. He said that he tried to call a couple of times, but you weren't home."

"I thought he was working."

"He is working."

"All the time."

"Well, no, he drops in quite a bit. We've got a lot of time to make up for."

Dana understood that Carson and Brady were

brothers. They would want to catch up, repair their relationship.

"Sit, let's eat. Dinner's ready."

Dana sat down and realized Carson was sitting in Brady's seat.

"If you married my dad, you'd be our mom for real," Karen said, looking in the direction of Carson as she stuffed a piece of broccoli in her mouth.

"Karen!" Carson said. He dished out two vegetables to Jean and then two to Ollie. "It doesn't work like that. Aunt Dana is already married to Uncle Brady."

"But it's not like they live together or anything. They can get a divorce and the two of you can get married."

Ollie looked up with anticipation. "You're getting married?"

"I'm afraid not, sweetheart," Carson explained gently.

"Why?" Ollie looked disappointed.

"Because Aunt Dana loves your Uncle Brady. And your Uncle Brady loves Aunt Dana. They're just a little confused now." Carson gave her a meaningful look. "But, eventually, we're hoping that they're going to work it out between them."

A knock on the door startled them all.

With a quick wipe of her mouth, Dana headed to the front door. "I wonder who that could be," she said as she opened the door, the cold hitting her full force.

"Hi, Dana."

Dana felt her heart plummet to her toes. God, he was beautiful. Even wrapped up in winter gear, he was beautiful.

"Brady, what are you doing here?" As soon as the words were out of her mouth, she wanted to take them back. He took her words of surprise as rejection.

He jammed his hands into his pockets and glanced over his shoulder as if he regretted that he had come. "Sorry. I didn't think this would be a bad time."

"Are you working?"

He looked down at his jeans and jacket. "No. Not tonight. I just wondered if you wanted to get a bite to eat." A burst of high-pitched laughter rang out, and Brady poked his head in to identify the sound. His face grew stiff. "Ah, I see you have company."

"No, no," Dana denied. "I mean, yes, I have company, but come on in. I'm sure there's plenty of dinner for you. Carson cooked."

He nodded. "Carson cooked. I should just go.

I'll catch you some other time.'' He turned to walk back to his truck, and unbidden, her hand shot out and grabbed the sleeve of his jacket.

"Come on in," she said, not wanting to sound as desperate as she felt. She gave him the biggest smile she could.

BRADY STEPPED into the house as if he'd never been inside before. Dana led him to the kitchen, with a quick glance in Carson's direction.

"Hey, look who's here to join us for dinner," she said brightly.

"Uncle Brady!" Ollie clapped.

"Hey there, Penelope," he greeted his youngest niece as he took off his coat. He draped it on the counter.

"I'm not Penelope. I'm Ollie!" the little girl chortled.

He dropped a kiss on Jean's head and then put Karen in a gentle headlock. "How are you?"

"Fine."

"How's the dinner?" He looked around the room for another chair, but there was none, so he leaned against the kitchen counter.

"Okay. Kind of dry," Karen said. "I like yours better."

Brady didn't know why, but that pleased him.

He glanced over at Dana who was looking everywhere but at him.

"Hey, you're in my seat," he told Carson in his best little-brother voice.

His brother shook his head. "It's mine now."

"I'll find another chair. There's one in the girls'—er—the guest room." Dana hopped up and strode down the hall.

"Now look what you've done," Carson chided his brother. "You've chased her away."

"I didn't do that," Brady denied, but it certainly seemed like he had. "You've certainly made yourself comfortable."

"The girls like it here." Carson wasn't responding to Brady's inferences. "The house is still a little foreign to them, to all of us."

"This is cozy," Karen put in.

Dana came back with a chair. Everyone scooted over to make room. The little table really couldn't accommodate a sixth person.

"Let me get you a plate," Dana offered. She heaped an enormous amount of food on it and set it in front of him. "Anything else?" she asked as she sat down.

"Just a fork," he said, but stopped her when she was about to pop up again. "I know where they are." He shot a sidelong glance at his brother, who ignored the look. He walked over and got himself a fork. Damn, he was being territorial over an eating utensil.

Karen was right. The chicken was dry. The girls kept up their end of the conversation and he spent most of his time trying not to look at Dana. The dinner finished as awkwardly as it began.

"Well, thanks," he said. "I'd better get going."

"So soon?" Dana asked.

"Yeah." If he didn't get out of there, he'd probably hit Carson. "Thanks for the dinner."

"I'll walk you out," Dana volunteered.

"Suit yourself."

WITH SOMETHING AKIN TO DESPAIR, Dana watched Brady shrug into his coat and head out of the house at a brisk pace. She had to run to keep up. She didn't want him to leave without at least a few private words. She didn't have time to grab her coat, but she still followed him outside. He was getting into his truck, the engine starting with a roar. He'd thrown it into reverse by the time she'd caught up to him and knocked on his window.

"Go in, Dana," he ordered her impatiently. "You'll freeze."

"I don't care." She crossed her arms and tried not to shiver. "I want to talk."

"I don't think there's anything to talk about," Brady said.

She swallowed back the lump in her throat. "Really?" She put a hand on his arm. "You don't think there's anything to talk about?"

He was silent.

"Can I get in?" she asked. "You're right. I'm freezing."

For a moment it looked as if he was going to say no, then he leaned over and opened the passenger-side door for her. She ran around the truck and got in before he could change his mind.

He rolled up the window and turned the heat on full blast.

"Thanks," she said. He was resting his wrist on top of the steering wheel, staring straight ahead. "So you don't think there's anything for us to say?" He was so close that she could easily reach out and touch his cheek. If she moved a few inches closer, she could kiss him.

"I guess there is one thing to say," he grunted. His eyes traveled over her face.

"Yes?"

"I hope you'll be very happy."

Dread crept up Dana's spine. "What do you mean?"

He didn't answer.

She pulled on his arm. "What do you mean you hope that I'll be very happy?"

He gave her a pained smile. "I know you've found your family."

"Found my family?" Dana didn't know what he was talking about.

"You'll go wherever the girls go. I don't blame you." He was speaking rapidly. "Carson's a good guy. And the girls love you already. I guess I always knew I was fixing up the house for you. That's probably why I put so much into it."

"Carson?" Dana was stunned.

Brady was jealous. Her heart soared. He thought she liked Carson. She hadn't ruined it all. Carson was absolutely right—they were just confused. She had married Brady to save the three girls, but she wanted to stay married to him because she loved him.

"Dana, if you don't mind, I've got to go." Brady gunned the engine. "Go back to your family."

Dana opened the door and started to slide out of the truck. She stopped and asked suddenly, "Do you love me?"

"That's not really any of your business."

"Loving me isn't any of my business?"

"I don't know what you want from me, Dana."

"I want you to say you love me."

"If that will get you out of my truck," he said. "Dammit. I love you. Now shut the door and go back to Carson and his three girls."

"We'll talk about this more," she promised, getting out.

"Not if I can help it. I'll have the divorce papers drawn up. Let's just agree to make it as painless as possible." He leaned over and pulled the door shut. The tires threw up gravel as he reversed his truck down the driveway.

Divorce papers. Ridiculous. Dana smiled though she was freezing. He loved her.

She walked back into the house, only to find Carson helping the girls put on their jackets.

"Did he leave?"

"He's jealous!" Dana whooped.

"I told you." Carson winked at her.

Karen came out of the bathroom. "Aunt Dana."

"Yes," Dana asked.

"You're coming for Christmas Eve and Christmas Day, right?" She looked anxious. "We're going to get our first tree tomorrow, but we're going to wait to trim it on Christmas Eve for Santa.'' She looked significantly at Ollie and Jean.

Karen's eyes had a mischievous glint. ''Uncle Brady's coming.''

''I'll be there then. With bells on.''

CHAPTER FOURTEEN

CHRISTMAS EVE, Dana sat in the living room of Carson's house. She was there only for Brady, and she'd formulated what she hoped was a foolproof plan. She'd spent the past few days running over Brady's last words. She knew who her family was. It was the stubborn man who decided he knew what she wanted.

She was married to him and a divorce was out of the question. If he wanted one, he'd have to fight for it, because she wasn't going to give in easily.

"I'm so glad you got here before the storm," Carson said as he walked in with an armful of firewood.

"Me, too. I didn't want to disappoint the girls by getting stuck." Dana watched Karen laugh as she opened a box of Disney ornaments. Ollie was throwing icicles over every possible surface.

Carson grinned. "Good thing we got three

packages of those. We're going to be lucky if one gets on the tree.''

"The lights out front look great," Dana commented.

Carson placed the wood into the fireplace to start a fire. "Brady came last night and helped me put them up. We're just going to have to take them down in a week or so, but it does make the place feel homey.''

Karen came over with scissors, a stapler and paper. "Aunt Dana, why don't you make the paper chains like we did at school. Dad—" Karen glanced at Carson, whose face went tender at her reference to him "—bought a bunch of construction paper just for that.''

Dana nodded as she took the supplies from the girl. It was good to have something to do.

"Don't make them too big," Karen instructed. "I want this tree to be perfect. Dad said he'd make popcorn and we're going to string them later with cranberries. Did you know you can get them fresh, not out of a can?''

A smile found its way to Dana's lips. "I didn't know that.''

Ollie and Jean giggled as they threw more icicles on each other.

Her hands barely fitting into the scissor handles, Dana started cutting strips of construction paper and asked Carson, "How's it going?"

Carson rolled his eyes. "I think you know. The anticipation for Santa is very high." He stacked the excess wood in the fireplace. The competent way he used his hands reminded her of Brady. He studied his structure and then stood up to find some matches.

"Tomorrow will be here soon enough."

He nodded, striking a match, and the fire caught.

"Should Brady be here by now?" Dana asked anxiously.

Carson shook his head regretfully. "Sorry, Dana. He called and said he had to work tonight. Someone called in sick." He leaned with one hand on the mantel, eyes studying the fire. "You know him. Work comes first."

Dana nodded. She did know him. But she also remembered a time when he put her and the girls before his work. They lapsed into silence and Dana worked diligently on her paper chain, trying not to let her disappointment ruin the evening. When the fire got going, Carson took out an old-fashioned popcorn maker. Jean, her tongue sticking out, carefully poured some popcorn into it. Then they all watched as their father shook the maker over the fire, deftly turning the basket so the kernels wouldn't burn.

Jean and Ollie clapped at the first pop, which was quickly followed by more. Karen hurried out with a bowl and the cranberries. As Carson emptied the basket of popcorn into her bowl, she said, "I think we're going to need at least three more baskets."

Ollie and Jean sat next to Karen, eating the popcorn.

"Don't eat that. That's for decorating the tree."

The little girls giggled and sneaked more popcorn, listening as their older sister explained the intricacies of popcorn stringing.

Dana watched her chain get longer. "How long am I making this?" she asked Karen.

Karen surveyed the colorful garland that Dana held up. "Oh, it's got to be a lot longer than that. It's got to wrap around the tree about ten times. It's a big tree."

Carson looked at her sympathetically. "I'd help, but I'm on popcorn duty."

"I think you'll have to make one more batch," Karen said. "Because Jean and Ollie are eating it all!"

Dana draped the chain around her neck and continued to cut the paper. Soon Carson's arms were straining from his job, the girls were string-ing popcorn, and Dana tried not to mind that Brady wasn't there.

BRADY'S TRUCK RUMBLED down the driveway to Carson's house, outlined by the bright lights they'd hung the night before. He'd spent most of the evening trying to figure out whether he'd come or not. Even though he'd spent most of his time trying not to call Dana, her face, her smile popped into his mind every other minute. But he wanted to give her the time she wanted.

The night he'd found her having a cozy dinner with Carson and the girls, he'd nearly grabbed her and kissed her. But he knew she wouldn't have welcomed that, though his spirits had been buoyed by the genuine confusion on her face after he'd told her to go back to her family. Then she'd asked if he loved her. If she was in love with Carson, she wouldn't have asked. Still, he couldn't shake the feeling that her question was really about those nieces of his.

If it wasn't, maybe they could start over. He'd decided to give her until the new year in the hopes that by then she'd have forgiven him.

His pulse began to race when he saw Dana's car.

He yanked three four-foot teddy bears tied with bright burgundy ribbons around their necks out of the truck. He walked up to the house and peered in the window. His stomach contracted at the sight of Dana sitting on the couch wrapped in a long paper chain. The living room glinted with icicles. Carson was in front of the fire making popcorn. The three girls were clustered between Carson and Dana, stringing the popcorn and cranberries.

So he was right. It didn't matter if he loved her. It didn't matter at all. Dana had found her family.

He didn't know how to curb the feelings of jealousy that stung him. She and Carson had a lot in common. And Carson had three things that Brady could never give her. Much as it hurt, he couldn't tear his gaze from the image in front of him.

He was about to turn around, when the door swung open.

"Uncle Brady!" Karen flung her arms around him and the bears. "Dad said that you had to work!"

"Well, it's Christmas Eve. I figured I could take a couple of days off, but I see that you're busy." Shoving the bears into her arms, he started to back toward his truck, gesturing to the cozy scene in the window. "It looks like your dad has company."

Karen's forehead wrinkled. "Dad has company?" She looked in the window. "Who? It's just Aunt Dana." Karen was bewildered. "You don't want to see Aunt Dana?"

"Well, she and your dad look, er, close."

"Where else is she going to sit?" Karen asked practically. "I don't understand."

"I'm not sure she wants me here."

Karen frowned. "You should ask her yourself."

"That's okay." He rested his hand on her head and gave her a quick peck on the cheek. "I just wanted to drop these off."

"You don't want to say hi to everyone?"

"N-no-o."

"Aunt Dana still likes you," Karen finally said, hiking the big bears higher on her hip.

What was the child talking about?

"She still likes you," Karen repeated. "Are you leaving because you don't want to love her anymore?"

"I never said I loved her in the first place."

"Yes, you did. You said it every time you looked at her. Any dummy could see that." Karen shook her head in exasperation and went back to the house with the bears.

Brady started heading back to his truck, when he heard Karen hollering. "Uncle Brady is here! Look what he got us!"

The scramble out the door was amazing. Jean and Ollie leaped down the short stairs and started to run toward him.

Brady turned the engine on. He'd just say hi and get the hell out of there.

"Can we ride?" Ollie asked.

"It's dark," Brady said.

Ollie and Jean looked so disappointed Brady leaned over and popped open the passenger door. The two girls climbed up and in. Ollie planted herself in his lap and asked, "Can I drive?"

Brady put the car in reverse and said, "Okay." He tried not to be distracted by the fact that in his peripheral vision, he could see Dana on the porch. He backed up and then pushed into first, grinding the gears. Damn. He hadn't ground the gears since he was fourteen.

Jean tugged on his sleeve and said, "Me, too."

"Okay. Ollie gets to drive to the road and back, then you do."

He felt even more self-conscious as they rode at two miles an hour up and down the dirt driveway. Each time they returned to the house, he stole a glance in Dana's direction. She looked wonderful, better than wonderful. She couldn't be in love with Carson. Not really. Not after all she'd shared with Brady.

DANA WATCHED as Brady got out of the truck with Jean and Ollie attached to him.

"Hi," he said with a quick smile directed at her, but he wasn't really looking at her. Jean and Ollie swung on each of his arms as they tugged at him.

When he smiled like that, he was hard to resist. If she didn't know better, she would have thought he was nervous. Part of her wanted to fling herself into his arms and the other part of her wanted to run and have him chase her.

"Hi," he repeated.

"Uncle Brady?" Ollie tugged at his sleeve.

"Yes?" He looked down at the little girl.

"Let's go in to wait for Santa."

Brady stopped, his eyes on Dana. Yes, he would go in. If Dana thought she wanted Carson, Brady would just have to remind her that she loved him. He had no idea how he was going to do that. But it was Christmas Eve. Anything could happen on Christmas Eve—even miracles.

Dana raised a quick hand and ducked inside the house, taking the garland off her neck. Why was it so hard to talk to the man she'd made love to?

"You're not thinking about leaving, are you?" Karen came up.

Dana looked down and realized that she had her purse in her hand.

"I thought you were going to stay and help us decorate the tree."

Dana put the purse down. "I am. I just wanted to move it. That's all." She had a plan and she was going to stick to it. Not that it was subtle. If she had to tackle the man and kiss him to death, she would.

"Good. I'm glad you're not going to start freaking out about how much time you spend with Dad."

"What are you talking about?"

"Uncle Brady. He thinks you like Dad. Why would he care? It's not like you're going to love Dad over him, right? You still love Uncle Brady."

"Yes."

"You can even spend the night. Since Jean and Ollie are too little to have their own room, we have a spare one. You can both stay!" Karen said. "It's Christmas Eve and we've got a lot to do if we're going to get that huge tree done by the time Santa arrives.''

"You might have to spend the night, Dana," Carson said. "That storm is going to be here soon. You won't be able to get back home."

"Yes, Dana. Spend the night," Brady said right behind her ear.

His voice seeped into her soul like brandy into her bloodstream.

"What about you? You have the longer drive." Dana felt herself flush from his intent gaze.

He shrugged. "There's the couch."

"Good!" Karen said, pleased with herself. "Uncle Brady, you can help Aunt Dana with the paper chain." She all but pushed them together on the couch, then rustled around and found both ends. She handed one to each of them. "It'll go faster if you work together."

"Yes, ma'am." Brady saluted his niece and Karen gave him a disapproving stare.

"I'll cut, you staple," Dana said. She held up the little scissors. "Unless you want to cut."

Brady gave a quick chuckle. "I don't think I could get a finger into those."

They worked in earnest silence.

Karen came up behind them and put her hand over their heads.

"What are you doing, Karen?" Dana asked.

"What do you think I'm doing?" she teased. "It's mistletoe. If I hold it over your head, it means Uncle Brady has to kiss you."

"I'm sure Uncle Brady doesn't want to—"

Brady's mouth descended on hers, muffling her protest. Dana went still, and closed her eyes, letting his lips explore hers. This wasn't the kiss of a man who'd decided to give up on his marriage. She might not have to tackle him after all.

"Take it to the porch," Carson interrupted, his eyes shining with approval. "We have minors in the room."

Brady leisurely pulled away, and Dana moaned in protest. He angled his head toward the front door. "So what do you think? Would you come to the porch with me?"

With her hand over her mouth, her cheeks bright pink, Dana nodded. She would go to the depths of hell with him. She'd promised for better or for worse. They'd already been through the worst. She sighed with pure pleasure when Brady led her to the front door. He grabbed his coat and put it over her shoulders before he pulled her into his arms. She laid her cheek on his chest and could hear his heart beating erratically.

"I'm not going to let you do it," he muttered.

"You don't belong with him. You belong with me. And if it takes forever to prove it, I will, even if that means I have to give you three girls of our own."

She smiled as she rubbed her head against his chest. "I am so sorry for everything I said. I'm not sorry I ever met you. I'm not sorry I married you. I'm just sorry that we've had to spend these last weeks not being with each other."

Brady was completely still and Dana wondered what he was thinking. Then she realized that it didn't matter. She had things to say to him. "You were right. I was wrong. These girls need their father. And I need you. Only you."

Brady put his hands on her face. "I'm going to miss the girls, too, but not as much as I've missed you." He dropped a feather-light kiss on her lips. "But I don't know if I'm enough for you."

"You are more than I could wish for. You're magic." She reached up behind his ear and as if by magic, produced her house key. "I think you're going to need this."

He grasped the key, then returned his arms to the position around her waist. "I was going to wait until New Year's. If you hadn't changed your mind about me, about *us,* by then, I was going to put you in a headlock until you agreed."

Dana smiled. "You can put me in a headlock later. Now I just want you to kiss me."

He lowered his head and whispered, "We need to make it good. We have an audience."

Dana didn't see the delighted faces peering out of the window at them because she had already closed her eyes. Love *was* magic.

The wait is over!

New York Times bestselling author

HEATHER GRAHAM'S

**Civil War trilogy featuring the indomitable Slater brothers
is back by popular demand!**

**It began with DARK STRANGER
and continues in November 2002 with**

RIDES
A HERO

The war was over but, embittered by the conflict,
Shannon McCahy and Malachi Slater still fought a raging
battle of wills all their own. A Yankee whose only solace
was the land she had struggled to save, Shannon hated the
hot-tempered soldier, a rebel on the run who stood for
all she had come to despise.

*Don't miss the opportunity to revisit these classic tales of brothers
who rediscover the importance of loyalty, family ties…and love!*

HARLEQUIN®
Makes any time special ®

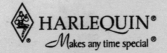

Steeple Hill Books is proud to present
a beautiful and contemporary new look
for Love Inspired!

HEARTWARMING INSPIRATIONAL ROMANCE

Love Inspired

As always, Love Inspired delivers
endearing romances full of hope, faith and love.

Beginning January 2003
look for these titles
and three more each month
at your favorite retail outlet.

Steeple
Hill®

magazine

♥──────────────────────────── **quizzes**

Is he the one? What kind of lover are you? Visit the **Quizzes** area to find out!

♥──────────────────── **recipes for romance**

Get scrumptious meal ideas with our **Recipes for Romance**.

♥──────────────────── **romantic movies**

Peek at the **Romantic Movies** area to find Top 10 Flicks about First Love, ten Supersexy Movies, and more.

♥──────────────────────── **royal romance**

Get the latest scoop on your favorite royals in **Royal Romance**.

♥──────────────────────────────── **games**

Check out the **Games** pages to find a ton of interactive romantic fun!

♥──────────────────── **romantic travel**

In need of a romantic rendezvous? Visit the **Romantic Travel** section for articles and guides.

♥──────────────────────────── **lovescopes**

Are you two compatible? Click your way to the **Lovescopes** area to find out now!

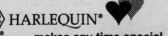

HARLEQUIN®

makes any time special—online...

Visit us online at
www.eHarlequin.com